BURNING BONES

T0158516

Miren Agur Meabe writes books for adults and children. In the course of her career she has received the Critics' Prize twice for her poetry collections, and the Euskadi Prize for YA literature on three occasions. Her novel *Kristalezko begi bat* (*A Glass Eye*, Parthian, 2018) and the short story collection *Hezurren erratura* (*Burning Bones*, Parthian, 2022) have been warmly received by readers and critics alike. *A Glass Eye* has been translated into several languages and received multiple awards. In 2020, she published her fifth poetry collection, *Nola gorde errautsa kolkoan* (*Holding Ashes Close to the Heart*) – which forms a triptych with *A Glass Eye* and *Burning Bones.* It won the 2021 Spanish National Poetry Award. She's a member of the Basque Academy of Letters.

Amaia Gabantxo is a writer, singer and literary translator specialising in Basque literature – a pioneer in the field and its most prolific contributor. Her essays and fiction have appeared in *Words Without Borders, The New Engagement, The Massachusetts Review* and *The TLS,* among others. She has worked in backpackers' hostels and taught at the University of East Anglia, the University of Chicago and the School of the Art Institute in Chicago. She's also a freediver.

BURNING BONES

Miren Agur Meabe

Translated from Basque by Amaia Gabantxo

PARTHIAN

Parthian, Cardigan SA43 1ED
www.parthianbooks.com
First published in Basque in 2019
© Miren Agur Meabe 2019
© This translation Amaia Gabantxo 2022
ISBN 978-1-913640-53-8
Editor: Susie Wildsmith
Typeset by Elaine Sharples
Cover design by Syncopated Pandemonium
Cover photo by Oihana Leunda
Printed and bound by 4Edge in the UK
Published with the financial support of Books Council of Wales and
Etxepare Basque Institute
Co-funded by the Creative Europe Programme of the European Union
British Library Cataloguing in Publication Data
A cataloguing record for this book is available from the British Library
Printed on FSC accredited paper

To Joanes, for the light.

PARTHIAN

CYNGOR LLYFRAU CYMRU
BOOKS COUNCIL of WALES

Creative Europe

Co-funded by the Creative Europe Programme of
the European Union

etxe pare
EUSKALINSTITUTUA
INSTITUTOVASCO
BASQUEINSTITUTE

This book is supported by Etxepare Basque Institute

I never travelled fast,
but I did travel,
the pain in my bones changes
every hundred metres
and no one knows the meaning of a kilometre like I do.
– Fabio Morábito

Remembering, rereading, the transformation of memory:
the alchemic gift of reinventing our past.
– Valeria Luiselli

Maybe they're dreams too, my memories.
– Joseba Sarrionandia

Contents

Miramar

Rats have been running riot here all winter. I start to itch as soon as I see the destruction: the broken ceramic dishes on the floor and the serviettes turned to confetti. Their tiny turds everywhere, little seeds of blood.

'Maybe because they ate salt?' my son wonders. 'The salt dish is empty.'

The transistor radio's cable, the matches, the scented candles we set on the table outside during long summer evenings, the aluminium paper; they tore through everything they found. A woven basket too, upturned on the floor. I give it a little kick, fearful that one of those beasts may be hiding in it and run towards my ankles.

'They're not around now, Ama, they come out at night. I heard them make a hell of a racket some time ago, on the ceiling... I've no idea how they got in. It's almost as if rats shape-shift their bodies into smoke when they smell food.'

'They probably found some leftovers from the last time you ate here with your friends. You don't even sweep up after you use the place,' I snap at my son.

'We should get a cat,' he replies, pretending not to have heard me.

It smells of damp and dust, of enclosed air. Multiple spider webs, thick as shoelaces, hang from the beams. Fragments and dust shed by the bricks inside the chimney have covered everything in a thin, copperish film.

'We shouldn't keep the place locked up like this. If we can't look after it between us, I'm going to have to sell it.'

1

Look after it between us. Who is this *us*. My son and I. I go on, braiding my rope of complaints.

'Expenses and more expenses, that's all this place is: taxes, electricity, water bills, and the maintenance it requires every year to keep it half-decent. Look at these walls, they're all chipped again.'

It's the saltpetre that causes them to bubble and crack; back in the day, masons used to mix concrete with beach sand.

'Careful on the steps. One of them is broken and the nails are sticking out.'

Coming here felt different before. Every time I come now, I have to run a rake through the place. I never write here anymore. Writing in the garden – that's a thing of the past.

'Ama, don't come into the bathroom.'

'What now?'

He steps aside to show me the toilet bowl. A huge rat has drowned in the hole.

'It must have been thirsty,' says my son, laughing. 'Get me something to take it out with; a piece of wood, or, better still, the shovel from the shed.'

'No, step away. I'll do it.'

I put rubber gloves on and grab the rat by its tail, but it slips out of my grasp and falls on the floor. It makes a sound like an oily balloon when it hits the tiles. I grab hold of it again, from the neck this time, as if it were a kitten. I throw it on top of the pile of stubble that I've been meaning to burn for months. My eyes and nose streaming, I retch.

My son leaves, taking the path that leads on to the street.

I stay there, looking at what used to be a vegetable garden, patches of sunlight falling on the grass. The sparrow-feeder collapsed under a mound of leaves, victim to some gale

2

wind. It seems to be saying that unless effort and desire work hand in hand, the weeds will smother every attempt at creating beauty.

I feel a gust of wind suddenly, a presence in the air: my mother picking strawberries for her only grandson; my uncle – my godfather – a man of sparse words and soft movements, planting flowers; my father taking an axe to the withered pear tree, to the barren vine, to the relentless ivy growing fat on the masonry wall, to the palm tree's unruly fronds.

The three silhouettes rise from the ground like threads of mist under the dirty March sky. In my head – like in ancient temples, where voices, sounds and notes swirl around cupolas – the voices of my elders mingle, saying words that were essential to them: asbestos, parsley, family, do, dimple, peas, lizards, geraniums, adze, seeds, harvest, water, everyone's, blooms, give. I'd like to erase them from the past, but the past is unreachable and all memory can do is attempt clumsy grasps with its treacherous nails.

We'll have to wait for more favourable winds before we build the pyre. We'll burn all the dead foliage, weeds and other remains – with soil attached to them still – and we'll spread the ashes of that fire over the flowerbeds and the roots of the fruit trees.

I close the door. The name of the property is spelt out on white-and-blue tiles to the right of the door: Miramar.

There are many other Miramars: the palace in Donostia, my friend's house in Valencia, a restaurant in Artxanda and a disco in Havana, a castle in Trieste, the inn in Naguib Mahfuz's novel *Alexandria*, and beaches, and cities. Homonyms, all of them. But this, only this one is my own. It's still here. And despite that, I can't help feeling that I belong here less and less.

3

I had a nightmare.

There was a swarm of squeaking rats under my bed, trying to climb up my sheets: their tails all tangled up, stuck together with some viscous substance. Packed into a swirl under the mattress, they bit and scratched the wooden frame incessantly, desperate to get out.

In Victor Hugo's *The Tower of Rats*, a whole village, turned into a pack of rats, kills Archbishop Hatto. In that instance, the rats represent a revengeful act against crimes committed by a tyrant; in mine, they represent disquiet. I hate them: back when we were kids we played in the rubbish dump and rats would always eat the pigeons we used to raise in the fort we built.

Like our fishermen like to say, rats live in their ships *nahizu-nahizu*, doing whatever they like. I heard one describe how, when he was a cabin boy, a sudden weight on his chest woke him in his bunk one night and, before he was able to open his eyes fully, a rat had bit him on the face. He got really sick, and when he started pissing blood the captain gave the order to head back to land.

According to *Advance*, a book containing naval surgeon Elisha Kent Kane's memoirs, rats became a grave threat to their ship when they found themselves trapped in the Arctic ice. The crew lit a fire in the bilge hoping the rats would suffocate with the smoke, but only a few died. They kept producing litter after litter, all of them hungry, as hungry as the fishermen themselves. The captain ordered the ship's fiercest dog be released into the hold, but it was all for nothing: the rats devoured its legs in no time. The crew had to cover up their ears to block out the dog's terrifying yelps. In the end some sailors managed to hunt down a fox and that worked, the fox cleaned up the relentless rodents.

4

At the ironmonger's they tell me that rat traps won't achieve anything, that I need to feed my visitors poison.

'It's more expensive, but it won't fail. If they eat it, they'll be finished within a couple of days. And don't worry, you won't even see them with their legs up and their bellies burst. They hide when they're about to die.'

The blue pellets that will bring this miracle about have the consistency of pork scratchings. I buy a bag and place them here and there, some on the ground floor and others in the room upstairs. I do it quickly.

I notice the crack on the ground as I walk out into the terrace; it gets bigger every year. The palm tree's roots are breaking through the paved area.

Damned palm tree, Dad used to say, *it's only because I can't do it on my own: if I could I'd chop it down right now.*

Grandpa planted it in the late fifties as a request from the owners. The land belonged to a rich family who used to visit in the summers to enjoy nature and the sea air. My grandparents looked after their garden plot in exchange for half of the harvest and the eggs the chickens lay. The sea-view is gone now; they built some apartments in front of it.

When I was a child the palm tree was as tall as me. I used to bring my friends over so they could admire it, because there were only half a dozen palm trees in the village. All of them planted by sailors.

When the heirs put the plot of land with the little house and garden up for sale my uncle decided to buy it; he wanted our family's bond to that land to endure. My godfather was a sensitive man. He had a set of shelves built in the upstairs room to host his collection of Caja de Ahorros Vizcaína books. He left the little estate to me. But I don't really have the will to restore this hundred-plus year-old house.

In the end Dad was right: the palm tree grew like a

mindless giant, and now it shakes its arms savagely when the wind blows. It scares me – what if they push roof tiles out of place, or damage the attic.

I need my little cosmos to be in good order. Bags, coats, keys – they can't just be anywhere. Each thing needs its place, be it a wardrobe, a cupboard or a box. I ask Adela to help me clean. She has been looking after another elderly man since Dad died, but she comes over often for a cup of tea and a chat. I've just moved to the house my parents used to live in.

'The changes are very noticeable, the house is not as full as it used to be,' she tells me. 'You've removed a lot of trinkets.'

'The Bilbao Athletic cups, the Basque ikurrina flags and the outdated encyclopaedias...'

'Old people like to keep everything... I miss your dad. Did you know that he'd get up in the middle of the night sometimes and come to my room? He would stand by the door, singing. I'd tell him off from the bed: 'Be quiet! The neighbours may hear you!' He would shrug his shoulders and say: 'So what, Adelita!' And he'd go back to bed in his usual cheery mood.'

'I have a question, don't you have a relative who clears forest floors?'

'My cousin, Nikolas.'

'Could he come to the garden house? I need to ask him a question about the palm tree. Tell him to call me, please?'

When Adela left I sat at my desk to organise some papers. I'm surrounded by Mum's porcelain dinner set, my uncle's stamp and coin collections, the ivory pieces Dad brought back from Africa. I feel overwhelmed by my worries. But I'll face them, one by one. The phone rings. The voice at the other end pierces my ear.

'Water is pouring down from your flat.'

It's one of my neighbours from my city apartment, the woman who lives downstairs. I change out of my pyjamas and then set out toward Solokoetxe, my neighbourhood in Bilbao.

The disaster happened in the bathroom. I feel as if I were made of plastic, a rigid, weightless material that can't stand up straight. Everything has taken on a brownish colour. How long must all that faecal water have been dripping through my house to reach the ceiling of the flat below. The stain is not that big, but it's definitely there. The putrid flow comes from above, apparently. The upstairs neighbours know nothing, there's nothing to see in their bathroom, there must be a crack in the sewage pipes. I clean my bathroom and open every window in the house. The stench won't let me sleep.

Rats are silent animals, nocturnal, scavengers, parasitic. Good jumpers. Quick, capable of climbing up straight walls. They can just as easily munch their way through cheese as through lead. They can swim for hundreds of metres and, when cornered, fight animals much bigger than themselves.

We are familiar with cockfights, but few know that there used to be rat fights too. Which rat came out the winner? The strongest, or the more thoroughly trained? And how did they train those rats?

They say cannibalism is common amongst rats: we too are capable of pushing through and leapfrogging over blood ties, moral reasons, common humanity and honour to ensure a win in our individual conflicts.

I kick the little house's door open. May the light get in and frighten those hairy fuckers. Even though they've eaten the poison some of them are still around, the floor is littered with their elongated little shits that look like oat seeds.

My son calls.

'How's the plague progressing?'

'Ever onward to victory... How are you, will you be coming over this weekend?'

While we're on the phone, I see two men approach through the door in the wall of the vegetable garden. I always leave that door half-open.

Nikolas and his boss are looking at the palm tree.

'What should we do?'

'It won't be easy to axe it down. We can't get a crane in here, there's no way into the plot. But we could do it with a scaffolding ladder and a chainsaw. We would have to chop the trunk down one slice at a time; it'll require a lot of patience. Palm wood is very, very hard, so much so it's almost impossible to burn. Afterwards we'd have to load the pieces into the van, and get rid of them in the authorised disposal centre... Many hours of work, señora. And we'll need special clothing too: palm fronds are very heavy and have these huge thorns in their undersides...'

'I don't want to axe it down,' I interrupt Nikolas' boss, 'but I don't want it to fall on the roof either.'

I don't know what to do.

'Take your time to think about it. We can prune it for now, clean up the trunk, get rid of moss and parasites. We're here to earn money, of course, but it's obvious that the little house and the palm tree make a beautiful pair. They were made for each other.'

He's right. Taking the palm tree from the house or a crown from a saint amounts to the same thing.

Nikolas rests a ladder against the trunk. He puts on a harness and goggles too. The boss leaves with a friendly 'see you later.' I start removing dead snails from my flowerpots.

'All these soft bits are rotten, it's better to remove them,' says Nikolas digging a hook into the trunk's fibres.

Sawdust falls off the trunk in a little downpour of soft, golden hailstones.

'Look, a blackbird's nest – but it's empty, it must be last year's.'

I'm not going to engage in conversation. I don't like people to prattle on while they're working.

'And who used to do these jobs for you before?'

'The men of the family,' I answer dryly.

My boyfriend used to help before, too. He was an expert handler of the telescopic scythe. He carried out difficult jobs like these for me many times. But that's all over now.

'Okay, now for the worst part, the crown. See those orange bunches that look like sprigs of wheat? Let's get rid of them, that way we'll hinder the palm's growth. Do you know that in some places they make honey and wine out of dates? That's a different kind of palm tree, though. Could you pass me the chainsaw?'

'Of course.'

'And move a bit further. These fronds are so heavy! Would you like to keep some? If you let them dry out we could place them on top of that iron structure you have over there and create a nice shady spot. What used to be there before, a vine?'

Bingo.

The chainsaw roars and the first frond falls. A second one follows. Then another. And another. And suddenly a stream of blood spurts from the crown. Bits of flesh and entrails splatter across the façade of the house. Nikolas leaps off the ladder.

A mob of rats escapes down the trunk of the palm tree, coming towards me. Others jump directly from the crown to the attic and enter the little house through the power lines. They know their way in.

I scream with my eyes closed, paralysed by terror. Nikolas

approaches and, holding my arms, shakes me to calm me down. After a while, when I see that there's nothing writhing or trembling in agony at my feet, my screams turn into sobs.

Sunday Apples

I'd like to let children speak and not push them out of the way,
but instead of doing that I exploit them, empty their pockets out...
– Stanislaw Lem

I remember the double-leaf iron gate in our hallway, the sandstone tiles and the wooden balustrade that went all the way up to the attics. We lived in an old house that my grandparents rented from some rich people in the village and this was why we had the privilege of a bathtub. With the economic prosperity that reached the town in the seventies, many homes soon displayed fancier bathrooms than our own.

Ama used to enjoy mentioning that.

'I used to bring my friends to look at the bathtub when I was a child,' my mother would say to highlight the poshness of our grand home.

We hardly ever used it, however. I was bathed every Saturday in the kitchen, in a brass basin that had been heated up on the stove plate. It was my godfather who started the habit of using the bathtub. At first the porcelain knobs squeaked and a thin, twisted stream of water flowed obliquely from the faucet, but a few turns of the pliers left it ready for service. When I grew too big to fit into the basin, I too found pleasure in that bathroom covered in pearly, hydraulic ceramic tiles decorated with geometric patterns.

'Come on, darling, you're using up all the gas,' Mum would say to get me to hurry up.

'You need to buy the kind of soap that makes a lot of bubbles, so I can bathe like they do in the movie *Sissi*.'

'But you're hardly dirty my love.'

Back then, my father worked as a mechanic in trawlers, going away for three or four weeks at a time in the fishing grounds of Gran Sol. Every time he returned from the sea, Mum would prepare his favourite foods and go to the hairdresser even if it was a week day. She had fine, greasy hair – which I inherited – and Dad teased her about it. I'm sure my mother also had plenty of reasons to look down on my father but mostly they liked each other very much.

Something happened, however, that sparked Dad's distrust. I had something to do with that, unfortunately, yet what I learned on that occasion may have helped me become a little smarter about what I hide and what I reveal.

One summer Sunday, my mother and I found a man in the square selling apples in the shade of the plane trees. She looked good in a green dress with white polka dots that complemented her tan.

'Would you like some apples, little lady?'

The apple-seller looked old to me, because of his grey hair.

'I can deliver them if you buy a whole box.'

'Should we buy some for Aitita?' Mum asked. 'Apples are good for people with diabetes; they're low on sugar.'

I nodded: little girls don't doubt their mother's wisdom when it comes to assessing the businesses they get into. So the man – let's call him Lucio – began to bring his apples home every Sunday. He'd knock on our door about four o'clock. My mother would leave the dishes in the sink, take off her apron, check herself quickly in the hallway mirror, and open the door. Lucio would drop the box in our storage room and leave after Mum handed over a bank note.

There was no shortage of compotes, cakes and jams at home. We appreciated the taste of Lucio's apples, their speckled skin and crunchiness.

One rainy Sunday, Ama offered Lucio a cup of coffee so he'd pause his deliveries while the deluge pelted the village. Lucio and Mum sat in the living room chatting with my grandparents about farm work and things like that.

When Ama walked him to the door, he whispered in her ear:

'It's such a shame for a woman like you to have a husband at sea.'

My mother frowned and closed the door on him without saying goodbye.

That afternoon she used the bathtub for the first time.

I had gone to the movies, but came back before the film was over because a boy in the row behind me put chewing gum in my pigtail, and my hair, ribbon and hairpins were plastered with it.

When I opened the bathroom door I saw my mother lying in the bathtub, in the dark. The light coming through the courtyard lit up her face with golden tones. Her eyes were closed, and apples floated around her, looking like bronze fists. She was muttering something I didn't under-stand: it's impossible for little girls to discern the meaning of certain words no matter how close they are when they hear them.

The cups trembled when my father kicked the sideboard. I'd rather forget it. Anyway, I want to make it clear that that outburst of anger didn't come out of nowhere.

He had just praised the latest tray of roasted apples, saying they were melt-in-the-mouth good.

'Out of this world.'

Looking at him sideways, I added:

'Of course they are, because last Sunday Amatxu bathed with them.'

My father's eyes suddenly looked like dark spiders. He

kicked the sideboard and went out into the street muttering something.

At night, in bed already, I heard the key in the lock and my mother's whimpers – she was apologising, I think.

The effect my comment had distressed me, but I think I made the accusation without malice. Or maybe not: maybe I needed to somehow expel the worm that the apple-man had lodged into my thoughts.

The next morning, Dad got up early to go to sea, like he always did. Mum looked sad, but they must have made peace because despite looking somewhat distant, he allowed her to give him a quick kiss.

As soon as he left, my mother filled the bathtub with ice-cold water, made me kneel and, pulling me by the hair, pushed my head into it. She pushed and pulled with gusto for quite some time.

Amour Fou

My mother must have been about fifty in that photo. She was smiling with her lips closed. She wore a blue blouse with satin stripes – a garment of discreet elegance, in line with her character. That photo had sailed with my father from cabin to cabin during his years of sea voyages, through countless stopovers in Durban, Rotterdam and many other ports.

He never disembarked, not even to take a taxi ride and get a panoramic tour of the city.

'I'm not interested,' he'd say. 'If you walk away, you may get lost.'

It puzzled me that a grown man might be afraid of getting lost because, as we'd been taught in school, even in the remotest of foreign places, asking directions would get you anywhere. I couldn't imagine what he meant. Apparently, some crewmembers frequented nightclubs while the ship was at port, and sometimes they had no choice but to ask the merchant company for an advance on future wages so that they could send some money home after squandering their most recent pay being entertained.

'My salary is paid in full every month, isn't it?'

Ama showed her gratitude by stroking his bald head.

I imagine my father lying on his cot next to a hatch that lets the cries of seagulls and the murmur of cranes through, his transistor radio's headphones on. The fan running. His wife's photograph on his chest. Knowing him, I'm sure that contemplating her image gave him the fortitude to stick to his vows. Every time he returned from a journey, the photograph spent the holidays on his bedside table, its glass misted over by remnants of kisses.

Shortly after my father retired, my mother underwent spinal surgery. For a whole month he stayed in her hospital room.

'I look at it as if I were doing time at sea. I don't care about the world beyond this ship.'

He took a toiletry bag to the hospital, which contained a razor. He ate all his meals there. In the afternoons, whenever I went to visit Mum's bedside after work, I'd bring over clean shirts and underwear for Dad. I often tried to persuade him to go home to sleep without making it obvious that Ama was beginning to feel uncomfortable having him constantly by her side.

It goes without saying that her husband's constant dedication was a huge comfort to her in the early days: not all husbands are so giving, or show their love so openly, nor do all husbands have such steady arms to offer for walks down hospital corridors. But there was an issue: his snoring disturbed the peace of the trauma floor and, after a while, my mother's roommate would give me looks whenever she saw me coming. A nurse warned me that some patients had complained.

What the hospital staff didn't know was that when it came to Dad, it was better not to press him: he was as sentimental and affable as he was stubborn and irascible. Going against his wishes led to reprisals: snappy responses, the thumping of tables, or vanishing for a few hours after slamming doors shut behind him. Afterwards we'd hear his key in the lock, and be on guard, but invariably he'd go to bed without even saying hello or having a bite. Most often he'd get worked up over nothing: if we interrupted him as he spoke, or were late for Sunday lunch. But, if we praised the squid in ink he'd cooked for us, that made him the happiest man in the world.

Whenever his holiday permit was nearing its end, our domestic bliss quickly deteriorated because Dad started to feel the pressure of his next departure, the stifling heat of the engine room, the slow motion of the calendar and his longing to be back home. Unfortunately, I have inherited that fiery temperament that kept us walking on eggshells at home, but with one difference: I am patient, I don't explode so quickly. My anger is a placated anger: I can spend days swallowing bile because I don't have the courage to say what I want to say. I owe that cowardice to him too, because at home we learnt to be meek, we acted like trained members of a choir.

'He's nuts,' I'd rule, unequivocally, hiding under a shield of indifference. My mother justified his behaviour:

'Don't say that! Have you ever put yourself in his place?'

And she reminded me that after the operation he had accompanied her to every physiotherapy session, and that he'd even gone as far as enrolling with her in the municipal swimming pool. If it hadn't been for Aita, she wouldn't have gone swimming half as much as she did. It was winter, the sports centre was far away and the pain pinched her every step. No, Dad was right there for the long journey, one small step at a time. They bought flip-flops together, and they wore their new microfibre tracksuits together.

Neither of them ever left the conjugal bed, a great sacrifice from Mum's part considering the sleeplessness Dad's snoring caused. They often got playful.

'The older you get the more I love you,' he'd tell her, while she tried to wriggle out of his embrace.

'Stop! You'll make me burn the béchamel sauce!'

The night before my wedding my father gave me some advice for the future: 'Never give up your position in the ship when the storm strikes. Hold on to your bed and think: "This ship is mine." If the other crew member does the same, calm can be brought about between sheets quicker than anywhere else.'

Years later, after Ama's death, Dad would take her photo as he sat on the bed to remove his socks, and say a silent good night. He had made it clear to me that he wanted to be buried with it.

'Don't forget: your mother comes with me.'

That request moved me, because I realised that the photo was like an amulet to him, a GPS that would guide him through the shadows.

For as long as he could manage on his own, he wouldn't accept hiring help. Until he tripped and fell and required a dozen stitches to the head and his arm in a sling. I took the opportunity to make a decision: I hired Adela.

The woman did not know how to stand still. In a few hours she made glassware, metal and windows shine; as well as my father's bald forehead, which she rubbed with aloe vera lotion. I had always thought that carers were the workers most prone to depression, but our house was lit up by the most happy-go-lucky person I'd ever met: the queen of nappies, the baroness of pedicures. Whenever I went to visit, I felt Adela had transformed my father into an elderly baby doll.

'I made croquetas and roasted apples, and a flan for an afternoon snack,' she said. 'He's got an appetite, your dad! And how he sleeps! If I'd let him, he wouldn't even get out of bed.'

So I paid no heed to my friends' warnings about checking receipts and all that, and did everything I could to make Adela feel comfortable, because it's not easy to find a person who acts both as carer and companion.

At noon they'd go out with the walker to eat *pintxos*. In the afternoons they'd play cards, go through photo albums, chop vegetables, and watch TV contests.

'But you abandon me at weekends,' my father protested. And he didn't sleep until she came back from her weekend break. And, as soon as she came through the front door, he'd snap at me:

'That's it, you can go now.'

That hurt a little because I was trying to be nice and do things like cook cod pil-pil or mussels in tomato sauce for him. But, objectively speaking, I must admit that I didn't spark him up like Adela did.

I think one of the reasons for my father's renewed enthusiasm for life was his carer's cleavage. She'd come into his room in her nightie in the mornings, fill a basin with warm soapy water and refresh him from head to toe, including his lower regions, while her breasts swayed to the rhythm. I wondered why she didn't dress properly for this, and her ambiguous ease around him bothered me.

I was stunned to witness their flirtation as I was about to walk into his bedroom once. Where had the enamoured devotion that Dad had always flaunted gone? It was the evidence of his desire that really upset me.

I swallowed saliva and entered. I asked Adela to cover up a little and scolded my father: how could he, always the gentleman, have these outbursts of senile frenzy? He shrugged and hummed a song looking at the ceiling.

When I told my son, he mentioned the Eros-Thanatos drive, something about the sweet madness that emerges when faced by the inevitable.

'Don't worry, Ama. Aitita could not be better cared for and, you know, at this point there's no chance you'll be getting a little brother.'

Not long after, he became seriously ill, affected by multiple pathologies. Adela and I took turns caring for him in hospital. Soon after, he began to stutter and lose his mind periodically. He would shout suddenly, his eyes rolling:

'Help! Bring a bucket! Water is getting into the boat!'

They explained that some heart conditions are associated with episodes of dementia.

'There's a rat! Kill that rat!'

He became incapacitated, unable to move by himself. Our daily routine was thrown off course. He stopped distinguishing between day and night. His pain spread. I sang songs he liked to distract him, like the one about the airplane that fell in the sea or the one about the pomfret fish; popular songs. At times, though, I had perverse thoughts: that his suffering was a delayed karma debt, owed by the pain he had inflicted on us while he was the head of our clan. I couldn't reconcile the reality of his delirium with Dad's personality; his terrified face seemed comical to me. All he did was call my mother, and try to sit up on the bed to go and grab her picture.

Adela was exhausted from his constant requests and sleep deprived, so she'd often lay down beside him to help him through the shipwrecks, plagues, and ghosts.

He died during my shift. I didn't expect it to happen then, and regretted my mistake in going to a high school reunion party the previous night despite noticing he seemed weak. Adela said that he'd spoken his last sentence that morning, that he'd told her: 'You've been a good woman.'

She at least got some sort of farewell. I was worse off, left with the eternal aftertaste of unspoken goodbyes.

It goes without saying that I made sure his will was done. I placed Ama's photo on his lap, between his folded hands and his new beret. When I kissed his cold forehead for the last time something from the past came back to me, a sense of Aita's habit of retreating behind walls. Fortunately, noticing the purplish stain the stroke had left behind his ear immediately drove away that troublesome feeling.

I have always associated what they call *amour fou* with stories of deranged lovers; with personalities who thirst for what makes them unhappy; with temperaments drawn to the cruelty of fate, to jealousy or a need for some sort of power; with the obsession of suicides who dream of subjugating death through the purity of their feelings of invincibility.

There were times in my life when I would have given anything to experience passion like that. But now, even though I know that lifelong love – that tiresome, boring feeling – does not come close to holding the charm of such unpredictable and immeasurable stories... what I wouldn't give in exchange for long-lasting, simple, calm adoration.

White Socks

Short white socks were part of the uniform. Our socks and shirts had to be white, like our hair bows. The sleeveless pinafore and belt, however, were navy blue. Because the fabric was made of thick wool, it required vigorous brushing to erase chalk marks and whatever stuck to us when sat on dusty floors to play card-trading games.

When I'd just started school, aged five, Sister Dolores scolded me for turning up without a uniform. The other girls were already wearing the prescribed pinafore dress, with all the folds carefully ironed, but I, following my mum's instructions, had to explain to the nun that my godmother had not been able to finish sewing mine yet.

She was good at sewing. However, due to her fragile health, she was unable to put the finishing touches to my uniform and I attended school in normal clothes. I felt like a black sheep in the middle of a herd of navy-blue clad girls, and looked forward to the day when I'd blend into the blue group and be safe from their looks of contempt.

And the day I finally premiered my uniform was memorable indeed, because I peed myself. In amazement, I felt the warm stream of urine sliding down my legs, released by inexplicable forces beyond my will.

I remember that the numbers zero to nine were written on the board and that the tip of my pencil had been broken several times as I'd tried to replicate them on a grid sheet. Most of the students had finished the task already, but I was still destroying my sheet with the rubber. I wet the chair while trying to overcome that crisis. It was a most unfortunate mistake: the rumour spread from mouth to mouth in the playground.

–So-and-so pissed herself... So-and-so pissed herself...

Once you earn a reputation for being *filthy*, your name and nickname get stuck to one another – like chewing gum and shoe.

Sister Dolores put a mop in my hands and I tried to clean the floor as best I could. After a short while, feeling sympathetic to my sobs perhaps, she sent me home to change with a few surprisingly tender words.

But I didn't take the road home; I went to the beach instead, thinking that I would be able to fix the dress that had been so hard to make.

It was a time of spring tides and there were more rocks than usual visible beneath the pier. The wind was southerly. I took off my socks and hung them from a protuberance in a rock. Then I lay down on the sand with my skirt up to my waist and the sun as my ally. Putting my faith in that natural remedy, I fell asleep.

I was being tickled: a dog sniffed my thighs and hit me with its snout. I was paralysed. I felt its paws on my chest, its drool on my forehead. Someone whistled from the dock and the disgusting creature disappeared, leaving me alone.

I picked up my satchel and left too. Amabitxi, seeing her goddaughter looking so pitiful and home before her usual time, put a pot of water on the stove to heat and fill the basin to bathe me, and hung the uniform from the clothes-line without giving much importance to the incident. I had returned wearing only one sock – I'd lost the other one at the beach – so they sent my brother to look for it. And he brought it back, dirty and misshapen, like a discoloured fish found dead on the shore.

A few years later, the nuns took us on an excursion to an orchard they owned near the lighthouse. We sang along the route. *Toma, virgen pura, nuestros corazones. No nos abandones jamás, jamás...* Take, Virgin so pure, our hearts. Never leave us, never ever...

The grass swayed, revealing pieces of fallen fruit. The crests of the hens looked like irregular plasticine shells. The sea. Someone said that the line of the horizon wasn't completely straight.

A man emerged from the lemon trees. He was old, scrawny, dark-skinned.

Sister Josefina explained that we were looking for flowers, as is the custom in May. He then asked for a volunteer to draw water from the well to fill the chapel's font. We drew lots and I lost.

'The gardener will help you just in case.'

Anton – if his name was Anton – was missing some teeth. There were missing bits in the well's shaft too, which gave me the impression that they looked alike. I peered down to look. I remember that a swarm of mosquitoes flew out, and one got in my nose and I sneezed. The gardener batted the insects away with his beret and pulled the tin bucket toward us.

'Loosen the rope and let the bucket down all the way, and when it's full lift it up slowly, without releasing it, otherwise the weight of it will drag you to the bottom. Mind you, you're not that small anymore...'

Both Anton and the well stank of dark swamp. The man leaned behind me and covered my hands with one of his own. I noticed his calluses. With his other hand he lifted my uniform. I didn't even move; if I did, one of two things could happen: either I fell headfirst into the well or I wasted the water that we needed to have blessed.

'You're such a beautiful little girl, just like this afternoon,' he told me softly. 'Even your eyes are the colour of honey.'

In my ears, his whisper mixed with the commotion of the girls walking into the chicken coop just as he squeezed my buttocks. Then he slid his hand toward the centre and, and then downwards. It was incredibly icky to think that he could have dirt under his nails, but, as I pulled the bucket, my muscles tensed up and pressed my flesh against Anton's finger. When I finished lifting the bucket, he growled and shuddered away from me. He disappeared among the fruit trees afterwards.

I grabbed the bucket and I went to where the others were almost blindly, so stunned that I waded into a mound of manure; I was up to my ankles in it. When they saw my socks full of ochre splashes, they burst out laughing and started making fun of me in a frenzy:

Filthy... filthy...

La Recherche de l'Absolu

I pick Nadine up at 4pm. The train is early and she's waiting already at Abando station. She has straightened her hair. And looks younger with her leather jacket on. She seems pale though.

'Are you alright?' I ask as I embrace her.

I've been running around all day. I just left a high school where I shouted my head off trying to persuade students that the book they'd read was worthy of a minimal degree of attention.

'I fell on the street,' she says. 'I have a wound on my knee and I just travelled all the way with my leg in a weird position.'

'Too bad. Let's go and get the car, we'll be by the sea in less than an hour. How is your baby?'

'Angry at me because I left her at home. Yesterday she got into my suitcase. She even scratched me. But she has to get used to being without me from time to time.'

Nadine is grateful for my interest in her cat. She tells me that Binoche ate something that gave her diarrhoea for days. That she put her in the bathtub to give her a wash, but the cat became so anxious that one of her claws got stuck in the drain. She almost went crazy not being able to get it out. It got very tense for Nadine too: as a child she'd often seen the limbs of lynxes or weasels clamped in traps that the animals themselves had torn off to save their lives. She had to call the firemen at three in the morning in the end. They managed to free the cat after injecting her with a sedative.

'Blessed be the firemen,' I said. 'Not only do they rescue

kittens from trees, they also rescue them from other compromising situations.'

'I had to pay for it, of course ... But what's good for my cat is good for me.'

'And your guy... What's up with him?' I don't remember his name.

'We met last week. I called him. We hadn't seen each other all winter.'

'And?'

'He had me for coffee in his apartment.'

'And?'

'I'm like a little girl. We were sitting on the couch and he suddenly said, "Are you afraid of me now?" And I said, "Why?" And he answered: "Because you're keeping your handbag across your chest." We ended up in bed, he's really nice, that's true, he always is, but he had a meeting afterwards, something he had to do... There always has to be a pea in the mattress.'

'Well, you'll have no problem finding a replacement. What does your daughter say?'

'Sophie? That I have to learn to give less.'

'That requires training.'

'I'm sick of men ... I don't want to hear the same lame excuses. I'll put up with my cat though, Binoche really does care about me.'

Nadine strokes a stranger's dog in the parking lot. Her love for animals is innate. She has a well-developed theory on the subject:

'When we were little girls, my mother would braid my sisters' hair; when it came to mine, however, she cut it almost down to zero. She hated my curls.'

She speaks without resentment.

'When something broke, the slap was for me, always,

even if it was someone else's fault... Yesterday was her birthday. I called her, but she didn't pick up. On purpose, I bet.'

'In every family there is someone whose role is to observe the others.'

'It's not that, she never accepted me. That's why I left home so young. Well, everything has a positive side. Herewith, the quick breakdown of many years of therapy.'

'The point is to be at ease with ourselves... Is your lipstick new? It suits you. I like it a lot. Will you lend it to me?'

Nadine closes her eyes. She sticks her arm out the window, toward the sunshine. The fields are full of overgrown grass and wildflowers and the clouds, vertical cirrus clouds, look like thin petioles. What else could anyone want. When we met, Nadine told me that she felt calmer around me.

'My animals saved me. I used to cross the meadow behind the farm and climb a fig tree. Although the sea was far away from us, it felt like I could catch a glimpse of the coastline sometimes. I spent hours imagining what it must be like over there, surrounded by my dogs and cats, chatting with them. It sounds like a bucolic postcard, but I was very alone.'

'I don't like animals. In summer my garden is full of cats and the cheekiest ones don't even get out of the way when I come in. I'm afraid of them really, I feel they might attack me.'

'Because you don't trust them.'

'Maybe.'

'My mother hates me because she never knew whether I was my father's or my uncle's daughter. I think I'm my father's; we look alike. But Mum dated them both for a while. She confessed this to me, she wanted to hurt me. The uncertainty of it ate her up inside, and it damaged me. She had to deal with her doubt and her remorse at marrying my father at the last minute, and not my uncle, her long-term boyfriend.'

'Are you telling me that two brothers competed for your mother?'

'They weren't brothers. My uncle became my uncle because he married my mother's sister shortly afterwards.'

'What a telenovela.'

'My parents broke up after a few years. Neither of them ever loved me. It's been hard for me to accept. He died recently, I told you, in an old folk's home. I went to see him, and forgave him. I haven't seen Mum in years... We can't be near each other.'

'And how is she with your sisters?'

'She acts normally with them. I don't see any of them anymore... I was sick as a child once and they called the doctor. When he examined me, he said that the strange hoarseness of my voice seemed peculiar to him; that it sounded like a purr. Then my mother lifted the duvet and a cat appeared – my hot water bottle, you know. She kicked it so hard that the cat never came back. Do you see what I mean?'

I have prepared the small room for her to spend the long weekend in. Nadine leaves a book on the bedside table, *La recherche de l'absolu*.

'*Mais l'absolu n'existe pas!*' I tease her. 'Are you still looking for the philosopher's stone? Nothing can turn stones into diamonds.'

'*Bon*, I don't want to lose hope.'

'Okay, I'm going to head to the supermarket. Why don't you rest while I do that.'

'Yes, I need to put this leg up. But first I'm going to call my neighbour. I left Binoche in her care. She'll feed her, change her water and clean the sandbox – fifteen euro a day.'

It wasn't a good idea: the lady decided to bring the

headset closer to the cat so she would listen to her owner, and the poor animal started to lick and nibble on the device desperately. I heard her sad miaowing too.

These days are a gift, says Nadine. The only downside is that she's uncomfortable, her stomach is giving her trouble: she's constipated.

We sleep late; we walk along the beach, cautiously, making sure she doesn't get her wounded knee wet; I cook fish for her and she prepares a *tarte tatin* for me. 'My real sister,' she calls me. I like to hear her say that.

She also shows me videos from an institution that protects animals that have been rescued from travelling circuses. She is very moved when she sees how tiger cubs that have known nothing but the bars of a cage all their lives react when they step on grass for the first time.

But the neighbour calls suddenly to warn that Binoche is barely moving. She says the cat is losing clumps of hair and hasn't pooed at all.

'She can't stand my absence,' Nadine said sadly.

'God knows what you'll find when you return! Remember that poem? A cat is left in an empty house not knowing where its owner has gone, or for how long, and it notices everything is as before but different at the same time. The cat is restless, incapable of taking the measure of its shocking loneliness... As a form of consolation, the cat starts to plan a very indifferent reception for the woman when she returns.'

'And where was the owner? On holiday, like me?'

'No... The owner was dead.'

'Then I must return as soon as possible. I couldn't possibly survive another rejection.'

Lord of all Saints

My grandfather asked me to touch the sores that the arrows of the Gentiles had inflicted on Saint Sebastian with my fingertips, one by one. He pointed out Saint Agatha's breasts laid out on a tray. And Saint Roque's puppy, licking the wounds on his legs. Saint Catherine of Alexandria wore an indigo velvet mantle. Saint Claire had the weatherworn skin of sailors. Saint Antolin looked up at the sky while a knife sliced his neck. Saint Michael, sword held high, crushed under his sandal a mangled being that reminded me of the snails we always ate on Christmas Eve.

The curls on those wooden figures, their leathery feet, the folds of their clothes, but above all, the infinite dignity of their faces, instilled in me such deep admiration that I assimilated their miraculous accomplishments with the same naturalness with which port children identified the different parts of ships.

When I went to see him at church, my grandfather would allow me to play some notes on the harpsichord in the apse and light a candle without throwing the corresponding coin into the box. In a drawer at the sacristy he kept a shoebox full of the tiny noses, fingers, ears, and fragments of robes of saints, as well as various other bits. He rescued these treasures from the altarpiece over forty years of sweeping the altar, and every single time he scrutinised the dustpan with the focus of a miner examining his sieve for a gold nugget. He kept the polychrome pieces in hopes that, should that magnificent work of art be restored one day, it would be perfectly complete again.

The church, with its luxurious props, felt like a stage to me and, my grandfather, its stage director. He was only the sacristan, but thanks to him, I thought, our family would have a direct path to heaven when the end time came. I imitated him and genuflected every time I passed by the shops on our street, every one of them an altar.

My grandfather spent the whole day in the sacristy preparing the liturgy or fixing things up. He would come home to eat and return to the church after a short walk. It was a habit of his to contemplate the orchards from the road while smoking a Rössli cigar. On one occasion, a motorcyclist ran over him in a bend and took off leaving him there. My grandfather wouldn't have said a word, but my mother noticed that he was limping. When she asked, he lifted the leg of his grey trousers and showed her an ulcerated wound. That injury never healed and, years later, as his diabetes worsened, his leg had to be amputated.

Ama called to tell me to go to hospital as soon as possible. She was undone: our beloveds' illnesses frighten us because we know that we'll have to go through them together.

'Aitita has lost his mind.'

His apparent lost mind was in fact transient dementia caused by low blood sugar. When I arrived in the emergency room, I was shocked to see him in a busy hallway, leaning against the wall like a vehicle parked in a hurry. He was trying (and failing) to sit up on the bed, very upset, whimpering and looking around for someone who'd say his name softly and help him calm down.

One of the effects of diabetes is that it consumes blood vessels; the same happens to plants when sap dries up. Poor circulation is incurable, so it sometimes requires drastic solutions: the patient's body may be cut down, left without arms or legs, like a pruned tree. Aitita's wounded leg was cut off on that occasion, and the other leg was cut off soon afterwards; both above the knees.

In the last years of his life, he'd often feel his legs under the plaid Scottish blanket and howl:

'This pain is unbearable! My legs hurt so much!'

Ama massaged his shoulders and explained that it was not a real pain, but a bad trick played by absent limbs, that it would pass in a few minutes. He would look at me in silence and I'd nod in agreement. I was very familiar with that kind of phantom pain ever since my left eye was enucleated.

Before the accident, my grandfather used to bring home a big black bag from the church. He always left it in the dark room. We gave it that name not because it had no light – there was a window overlooking the landing – but because we kept all sorts of things in that long, narrow space. Three cupboards dominated the space as you walked in: one where the preserves, jam jars, and bags of nuts and legumes were arranged in neat rows; next to it, a three-door wardrobe where we kept discarded clothing and footwear, including Aitita's spare cassock and chasuble; and, in the back of the room, the shelves for linen overflowing with sheets, towels, tablecloths and kitchen towels.

Randomly on the floor were: a wine carafe, a brazier, a toolbox, a sack full of our old toys, jelly sandals, and other things I don't remember. There were strings of garlic and dried peppers hanging from nails on the wall, rain jackets, a carpet beater, a scoop net, a bristle broom to wax and polish the floors, and a fly swatter. And hanging from a coat rack, the mysterious black bag that no one but my grandfather was allowed to use.

The dark room was a mysterious laboratory that stimulated my senses. More than once I managed to take a sip of the sweet wine hidden behind the box of shoe polish. However, I had not yet discovered the secret of that bag. All I knew was that every now and then they knocked on our door and Aitita would go out carrying it under his arm.

One day when I asked my grandmother what was in it, she replied that it was church property.

'Church property? And what is it doing here?'

The bag did not even remotely resemble the embroidered tablecloths, alpaca chalices, or finely embossed reliquaries that my grandfather kept so neat, perfect and shiny in the sacristy.

'Because, if it's here, Aitita has it at hand if they call at night.'

'But what's inside?'

'The Holy Chrism.'

Useless clarification. Back then children didn't receive many explanations.

One night, my grandfather and I were left alone because my mother and grandmother were caring for Amabitxi, my godmother, who was admitted to a clinic. We had vermicelli soup for dinner. He then did the dishes and I climbed on the bench to cover our goldfinch's cage with a napkin.

I hadn't fallen asleep yet when the doorbell rang. The front door had a large peephole with rotating vanes that allowed a comfortable view of the landing. A woman was asking after the sacristan. Aitita walked towards the door.

'On such-and-such street, on such-and-such number,' she said before leaving.

My grandfather put on his spare cassock and took off with his black bag.

'You, go to bed. I'll be right back.'

As soon as he came out, I grabbed his lace vestment from the wardrobe of discarded clothes and placed it on top of my pyjamas. It reached to my heels. Suddenly turned into an altar boy, I hurried down the stairs.

It was quite a stretch from our house to the fishermen's neighbourhood, but I was no stranger to it as my nanny's family had a tavern there. The wind shook the clouds, nimbus that looked like bread dipped in squid ink. I followed my grandfather's hunched figure from a distance through the cobbled streets. In a corner, he bumped into a drunk. I heard him scolding the man.

When I caught up with him, he raised his arms in astonishment and quickened his pace.

'I hope you won't regret following me,' he sighed. 'Take it, take it yourself.'

And he put the black bag in my hands. At that moment I felt so terrified that the thistle flowers hung to dry in the lintels of windows looked like bats to me.

The woman was waiting for us where she said she would be. We followed her to the third floor up a narrow staircase. Inside, a curtain separated the hallway from a tiny room where there was a bed with a spindle headboard and an old woman on it.

She kicked her legs under the quilt. Her head was drooping, but the woman who had rung our doorbell – her daughter or daughter-in-law – was determined to comb her hair. On the other side, a man was squeezing the dying woman's hand. There was no other decoration but a rosary with beads big as plums hanging from a lamp. My grandfather signalled me to kneel. I found an old sweet in my pocket and put it in my mouth.

I was finally able to clarify the mystery of the bag when the priest arrived a bit later. There were two silver instruments inside: a cylinder with a cap and a matching case with engraved designs. Aitita took gauze from the case and, uncovering the liturgical cup, dipped it with very clear oil. He then passed it to the priest, who traced the sign of the

35

cross with it, first on the patient's forehead and then on the back of each of her hands as he muttered some words. The old woman's throat made a sound like a rusty swing set. My grandfather sent me out.

At the end of the corridor was a frosted glass door through which I could see some dim light. I went there and flicked a switch. A herd of cockroaches scuttled to hide under the firewood. A figure sitting in a huge crib looked at me.

He was a boy with a face filled with pustules. My heart skipped a beat. He swayed and drooled, calling his grand-mother with a faint whine: 'Amuma, amuma...' He stretched his arms out towards me.

I didn't know what to do. I showed him my empty hands. His crying became louder, and tears made those hard, bar-nacle-like crusts on his face shine like flames.

Then I noticed a jug on the stove. I poured a few drops into my handkerchief and repeated the rite I had just wit-nessed in the other room with the boy. He relaxed. Then I took the sweet out of my mouth and put it in his. He lay down slowly in his giant crib and kept very still.

I went down to the hallway very quietly and sat on the step waiting for my grandfather. It was dawn when my grandfather woke me and held my hand to help me get up. I felt like a fish released from the hook too late.

It's raining in the cemetery. We are standing, huddled next to a pile of soil that looks like pureed lentils. We surround the family, shocked by the unexpected tragedy: a lorry ran over a classmate. There is a buzz: we are a hungry swarm.

Aitita offers the thurible to the priest, who swings it over the coffin three times. The rain has formed a puddle in the pit, and a toad splashes inside it. The undertaker throws a shovelful of earth. The animal tries to climb but slips back to the bottom.

I remember the boy I met at the dying woman's house, and also the martyrs, always so lonely and so alone, and it occurs to me that someone should help get the toad out of the hole, but no one does anything, not even me. We watch the coffin be lowered and crush the toad, and the flowers that fall and keep falling, and I think to myself that thank goodness my grandfather is the Lord of all Saints because thanks to that, we at least will be saved.

My First Thanksgiving

There is a wind rose on the Santa Barbara pier. The dock is a long wooden breakwater erected on sturdy piles nailed to the bottom. It starts from the avenue and separates the beach into two halves bordered by rows of palm trees on either side. On the port, squadrons of black pelicans flock around the boats as they arrive, grunting and squawking.

Several buildings are grouped in the central part of the pier, all with white window frames. Seen from a distance, it looks like an idyllic fishing village, but it is a complex of restaurants, ice cream parlours, trinket shops and booths selling trips to the Channel Islands Nature Park. The photos make you want to get on a boat to go sighting grey and humpback whales.

The wind rose is at the end of the port, chiselled on the wooden floor planks. I have twice placed myself in the centre of that symbol, on the two occasions I've visited the city, surrounded by the initials representing the cardinal points, standing in the sun, eyes closed and forehead raised as if I were in the crossing of a temple waiting for a ray of light from the heavens.

Some people need to eat the same fish twice. I don't know whether that happens because in trying to satisfy our hunger we always pull our net from the same waters, or if it's because the tide only ever gives us what it has reserved for us.

Iris Ferretti invited me for dinner at her house in a colonial-style townhouse development. I wouldn't have minded staying by the hotel pool with my pen and my jet lag, but she thought it was rude to leave me alone on Thanksgiving.

I had arrived the previous day to speak at a convention. It may seem glamorous, but, to be honest, I have my doubts about the real scope of this type of activity, so I take travel as a reward for the many injuries that come with my profession.

I showed up at seven with a silk scarf for the hostess and a couple of bottles of wine, one red and one white because I didn't know what to bring. Three of her colleagues were already in the room: Margaret, a professor of criticism; Dave, a researcher on minority languages; and Ainhoa, a young woman who taught Basque language and culture and felt familiar to me, I couldn't figure out why.

'I hope you didn't cook a turkey,' I teased as I greeted Iris with two kisses.

'Impossible. I had to take my son to the doctor. He's unwell, ate too much ice cream... How are you?'

'It's nice to be here.'

'It's lucky that you came at this time. Today is a special day. Take a seat wherever you like.'

'Is it always on the 25ᵗʰ?'

'No, it's on the fourth Thursday in November,' Margaret said. 'You might know that this holiday has its roots in an English custom. Well, the French also celebrated the end of the season in Canada. There is a striking painting by Jennie Brownscombe, *The First Thanksgiving at Plymouth*, in which the settlers are depicted sharing their food with Native Americans...'

Dave cut in:

'Or is it the opposite? I know that painting: an idealised representation of a picnic, a complete falsehood. Initially the colonisers had nothing to eat, and only survived because the natives gave them seeds and taught them to fish.'

Margaret pretended not to hear.

'The Native Americans appear to the right of the painting,

sitting on the grass, watching the community. The whites bless the table. There are two or three chiefs among them, with their feathered headgear and all—'

'Excuse me,' I interrupted, 'these canapés are delicious. What is it, tuna?'

'Ainhoa brought them.'

'Santa Barbara bites: tuna cubes mounted on a mix of shrimp, avocado and octopus. They sell them at the Fish House on the promenade.'

Dave continued:

'We already know how that coexistence evolved: the pressures to cede territories, the heads of the rebel leaders on spikes, their descendants sold into slavery.'

Margaret snorted, and I turned the conversation around to ease the tension between the two colleagues.

'Back home we make a stew with tuna, potatoes, onions, peppers, garlic and tomatoes: it's called *marmitako*.'

Dave made a gesture with his mouth, annoyed with Margaret – or with me, perhaps, for interrupting the conversation again.

'The dish takes its name from the pot; the *marmita* pot fishermen used to cook on their boats. It's very easy to prepare, isn't it, Ainhoa?'

'No idea.'

'If someone lends me their kitchen, I'll happily cook it any time.'

'We could go tuna fishing on my boat,' Dave said, suddenly excited.

'Great plan.'

I'll confess, whenever I'm in good company – more so if we're sitting around a good table – I over-share. Divulging the juicier parts of your private life has the added benefit of turning casual interlocutors into friends.

The first time I visited this city, I had the feeling that

even homeless people were happy sleeping on the benches of State Street.'

'You're right. The good weather helps lessen the drama.'

'I found everything the same, or almost the same. Do you know what I did yesterday, as soon as I arrived? I went to the port to see the wind rose.'

'Is there a wind rose in the port?'

'It's hardly visible. It's really worn... Time is merciless.'

'With everything and everyone.'

'The thing is, back then I was going through a bad spell, stuck between two loves...'

Iris laughed and raised her glass to make a toast.

'Welcome to the club!'

'And years later, here I am in the same spot again.'

'But not with the same two, right? Tell me you're not dealing with the same characters,' Margaret asked, her eyes wide.

'No, please.'

'And so, you feel that the wind rose of Santa Barbara guides you and hints at the course you should take...'

Dave's tone was ironic. However, it was Ainhoa's high-pitched voice that surprised me:

'You've never been any good at choosing.'

I felt my dining companions' curiosity like darts pointing at a target.

'You weren't any good at it when you interviewed me for that job. I was a newbie, but I needed the job more than I needed breathing. I basically went down on my knees...'

Surprise.

More than once I've thought that if all the people I harmed while working at my old job were to arise like zombies from the twists and turns of my memory, the shame would eat me up. In my defence, I'll say that selecting candidates was difficult since, in addition to the objective data (misspellings, incorrect pronunciation, shallow answers), my first impressions of the candidates' personalities (know-all, clueless, wallflower) played a part in things too.

'I don't remember why I rejected you, I'm sorry. If it's any consolation, that company was not exactly paradise.'

Iris began to knead breadcrumbs. Margaret cleared her throat. Dave pulled a pack of tobacco from his shirt pocket.

'So I heard. And anyway, it doesn't matter. As you can see, I moved onto much better things.'

Dave went out to smoke in the garden. The lit tip of his cigarette waltzed among the bougainvillea and a gust of warm air filled the living room. I unclipped my hairpin to hide my discomfort.

'I'm glad, Ainhoa.'

The tuna leaped around in spasms.

By the time we got out of the harbour, the Mexican man who helped Dave with the maintenance of his boat had taught me how to put the bait on the hook. We swung the rods over the stern as we left the shore behind. We had travelled several miles when I felt the pull. I struggled with the rod between my legs. Dave, who was at the helm, slowed down.

'Hold on,' he warned me. 'Hold on, be careful not to break the fish's lip. It would escape.'

The fish finally gave up. I pulled it up and Orlando used a hook to catch it under the gills and bring it on board. The tuna convulsed for a while with dull thuds. Orlando cut off its head with a machete in one fell swoop, twisted it, and pulled it off, ripping off its viscera, a voluminous scarlet dangle. Blood splattered the old canvas sail spread on the deck.

The rest of the morning went by chatting and snacking. I took some notes too: thinking outdoors makes me feel good.

Dave showed me the control panel in the cockpit and winked at me.

'Let's see what this compass tells you.'

I liked his gesture of complicity.

In the afternoon we sailed by Anacapa, a volcanic island made up of three barren islets. The cliffs plunge abruptly into the sea, like basalt blades. Saffron stripes glistened on the hills, coreopsis bushes. Dave explained to me that the toponym comes from the Chumasch language and means 'miracle island or mirage island.'

'There are hundreds of caves, but it's a bad idea to get close unless you know the reefs well. This coast is more treacherous than it seems.'

'Can't you visit?'

'There's a path across the rocks from one end to the other of the island, but that's for people who are not afraid of seabirds: they can't stand intruders in their domains.'

I picked up the binoculars to look out over the sea. Maybe I could see some petrels.

Then came a loud splash: a whale had emerged with its young near us. The rubbing of those bodies against the water felt like a symphonic chord, the most natural and euphoric harmony ever. I said thank you in silence.

'How long are you staying?'

'Another four days. I want to do the mission trail.'

'Why would you want to do that?'

'I had a book as a child, called *La cruz y la espada...*'

'I see. Missionaries; assassins in soutanes at the service of the empire.'

'Aren't you exaggerating a little?'

'The missions were a tactic to subjugate the territory and fund cities. They became extermination camps under the pretext of being places of salvation for the infidels. The atrocities and outrages committed in them have not yet been brought to light. How could the natives not shoot arrows of fire at them?'

'I shouldn't tell you that the founder of Santa Barbara was a Basque Franciscan father then. I just read it in a tourist brochure.'

The siren of the lighthouse and its dim light mingled with the thumps of Orlando's machete as he sliced the tuna.

As soon as I arrived at the hotel I saw I had an audio message on my mobile phone.

'It was you. I knew right away. I was riding waves on my board and a seabird appeared. Its beak was very red, the colour of your lips. It stared at me sideways, with its right eye, like you do. We don't get birds like those here, it was different. I'm sure it came from where you are. You sent it to me so I won't forget you.'

I thought: sometimes it's better to remain silent.

We met in Dave's studio. Below, the prattle of children playing on the promenade where couples paraded on bicycles, bohemians displaying their trinkets and skaters flew by in tropical attire. A homeless man with a very long beard built a sand sculpture right under our terrace.

Iris and Margaret had arranged an assortment of colourful sauces on the table. Ainhoa watered the plants. It seemed to me that all her resentment towards me had dissipated. Orlando had joined our group and was humming a song on the guitar, leaning against the railing. Dave served mojitos and I distributed the food in clay bowls on a tablecloth with a macaw pattern.

'A Lekeitio recipe,' I said happily. 'Bon appétit.'

Spoons sank into the broth.

Margaret ran to the bathroom and Iris sank her face into a bucket. Orlando put ice in his mouth and Dave swore out loud. Our oesophagi were in flames.

Ainhoa stared at me, reclining in her rattan chair. Saying nothing, she got up and left, her sandal's heels resonating on the flagstones. Dave rushed after her. The car engine roared out of the garage.

Then the wind blew, causing the parasol to sway. A gust of sand made a mess of the table and we all started muttering excuses to leave.

'Monday in Classroom 9,' Iris mentioned as she said goodbye.

'That girl's a little crazy,' Margaret whispered in my ear, then asked Orlando, 'Can I give you a ride somewhere?'

They leave me alone.

I empty the contents of the pot into the toilet, put the sauces in the fridge and walk out to the terrace to pick up my handbag. Then I hear the key in the door.

The gale storm has driven everyone away, and the edges of the sand sculpture on the beach are blurred, a battered compass undone by the winds. Dave comes close and wraps his arms around my shoulders as we watch it vanish.

Tesserae

And the places of memory shone
like tesserae torn from a golden mosaic.
– Martin López Vega

We are sitting on a stone bench next to a big house on the road to Karraspio beach. My mother knits and my godmother flips through the pages of a book. I pluck leaves from a plant and spread them on a rock, like fabric on a counter. I prick them with a knitting needle. *Kontuz, laztana.* Careful, darling. I want to embroider on the sheet, engrave on it, write. Sun beams through the plane trees.

Kontuz when riding a bike, don't be too rough lest your hymen tear. *Kontuz* not to lose your notebook because someone might find your thoughts inside. *Kontuz,* mind the wolf and its many shapes: marijuana, slot machines, girls and boys who know too much. *Kontuz* not to catch leprosy like Ben-Hur's sister did. *Kontuz,* your wings might melt if you fly too high. *Kontuz* because the birds might eat your crumbs and then you won't find your way back home, and then you'll be lost and alone in the streets.

We play in the street, around the fountain in front of my mother's shop and in the nearby alleys. In winter we put on plays. We wrap coats around our faces as if they were mantles. *You be the shepherd, she the angel, you the ox and you the mule.* The manger in the archways. I want to be Maria, but for that you must pay a peseta to the older girls. They, however, seize my doll for free and have her play the part of baby Jesus.

In the cinema, a doll with a burned face in *The Tree of Life*. Crazy Elizabeth Taylor sets fire to her house. I recount the movie at dinnertime. My grandmother speaks with her hand in front of her mouth. *Our sister got burnt as a child too. The rest of us were in the cornfield with our mother, she'd left the little one watching over the hearth. Her skirt caught fire. A neighbour saw it and pushed her into the well. First she burned and then she drowned, the poor thing.* Every night I imagine a girl my age by my bed. When I open my eyes she lights up like a torch.

A group of women light the bonfire of San Juan on the roof of the municipal water tank. We dance in circles. I fall and T. wipes my knee with some lemonade. *If we could jump over the fire, where would you go?* Her dress gets dirty and I rub the stain with lemonade too. *To heaven. And you?* My friend's eyes are fireflies at sunset. *To Bambi's forest, with you. And we won't take any boys along.*

The boys rip out the legs of crabs. The boys shoot rats with their air guns. The boys throw snails and slugs into the fire. The boys murder the pigeons in the square with slingshots. The boys slice lizards' tails off with their pocket-knives. We are crabs, rats, snails, slugs, pigeons, lizards for the boys. When we flee from them, we take refuge in my mother's shop.

My mother says that it's only right to add a few extra cen-timetres of free fabric to her loyal customers' purchases. The ladies buy tulle veils to go to mass; the girls, white cloths. I sometimes see white rags like those soaking in a basin filled with water and bleach, in the sink. But the water looks reddish, as if wine or red fruit liqueur had fallen into it.

My grandmother and aunt leave wearing black tulle veils, but they return in a hurry, frightened. They pray in the kitchen. My father closes the shutters. My mother takes out the Parcheesi board and pushes my brother and me into the dining room. *Don't move and don't make any noise.* Gunshots. Hours under siege. When they finally let us look through the shutters, we see blood in front of our neighbour's door and shrapnel impacts on the walls. Someone's left a bunch of flowers on the ground.

The satin flowers on the wallpaper float among the snow. My godmother's words are snowflakes that dissolve almost before they are uttered. I lie down next to her when I get home from school so she'll read to me. She asks that I repeat some excerpts. *Bring me the jewellery box.* Pearl earrings, a rosary with emerald glass beads, a small medal with an inscription: *October, fidelity.* She puts a ring on my finger, an amethyst. *For you, when I'm gone.* Purple is my colour from then on.

Dasha's jersey, its rhinestone-studded neckline, is also purple. The Cossack princess appears on the track holding the horse by the reins. Someone says that the musical accompaniment is from *Dr Zhivago.* Dasha whispers something into her horse's ear and it whinnies as she rides. Not today. Today is daylight and we find her sitting on the steps of her caravan and she doesn't look like a princess to us. She asks us to buy her a packet of Piper. In exchange, we'll get a menthol cigarette. Since we're in a rush, we don't let Maritxu, the tobacconist, do our eye make up in her back room like she usually does and we smoke our cigarette on the shipyard ramp, under the starry sky.

The circus saddens me despite its many stars. The boys hunt cats in potato sacks rubbed with grease, or with the bait they prepare by crushing anchovies and pieces of glass. Three tickets per cat. Tigers swallow them in one bite, these delicacies, while they're still alive. The straw on the cages changes colour and the horses, fenced in, roll their eyes back and kick the air. My godfather gives me a free ticket because he works in the town hall and the performers always give them a bunch. *Taxes and dues.*

My godfather burns magazines and mementoes on the stove. The other night Civil Guards knocked on our door. They were looking for a young man, but they got the wrong house. He was out of sorts for several days. We keep an ikurrina flag and a fronton paddle decorated with illustrations of Basque dances hidden in between the living room curtains. The silver bracelet he brought me from Biarritz has seven coats-of-arms, for the seven provinces. *I'm going to burn the letters too, just in case.*

Mum writes letters in her shop. She draws a small cross in the header, before the date. *What's written down remains forever. Be careful with what you write, child.* I do my homework leaning on the counter. If I have a writing assignment, I draw a cross in the header like my mother does. When she has news about people whose names she doesn't want to write, she uses only their initials.

The trimmings have initials: J H S. We ask my grandfather to give them to us to ward off hunger pangs. He gives them to us in newspaper cones. He says he usually gets twenty-five holy wafers from each sheet of wafer paper; he cuts them with a puncher, one by one, and saves the leftovers for the children. We line up under the park's magnolia tree to eat them, but the boys twist my arm and steal our snack.

Sometimes, we earn another snack carrying water for the churro stand. We pair up to go to the gas station behind the church and fill the bucket with a hose. It's hard for us to transport it, and we imagine the water is filled with millions of beetle-like insects with hairy antennae. Microbes. Luckily, the churrero doesn't have a microscope. He used to reward the errand with a round, flat, sugarless churro that looked like a slug. Not anymore though, because of Koittadua.

Koittadua follows us everywhere. He is a big, gangly fool who lives with his mother in a basement. They only have one street-level window, and the hatch is always open. From the street you can see a square room that's both kitchen and bedroom, all in one. The mother sits all day in a little bulrush chair, busy with sewing jobs. She doesn't look like our mothers: she wears damascene earrings and hair combs. Her son peed into the churro stand's bucket. The older boys made him do it: either he did it or they'd tell everyone his 'secret'.

The secret was that he was caught choking the snake near the convent. We didn't see it, thank goodness. That's why he had to piss into the bucket, and that's why the free churros ended. Now he lives in a hospice. Some older boys sent him into an orchard in Arropain to steal chickens. One chicken, two tickets. The farmer threw the dogs at him and Koittadua turned up in the town square upset, flustered, his tibia in full view and a smothered chick tucked inside his vest. They say he doesn't get out of bed anymore.

My aunt and I sleep in the same bed. The bed throw has a red flower pattern. I squeeze against her back. I inhale the cinnamon in her hair, Sultana lotion. In the mornings she brings me an apple to bed before breakfast. *Don't get up yet, it's colder than the sea of penguins.* Noises in the kitchen. *I have to tell you a secret, Auntie: I don't want Saturday to arrive because my brother returns from boarding school then and makes me drink vinegar in the dark room.* She laughs; she doesn't understand me.

My aunt doesn't talk much, although she laughs loudly. She only knows one story, the story of the fox that fooled the wolf: the fox made him drink all the pond water, telling the wolf that the moon he saw reflected on it was a talo flatbread. But it was the moon. The wolf drank all the water for nothing. My aunt deepens her voice at the end of the story, when the fox removes the cork he'd put in the wolf's backside. *The amount of water that came out! So much so it flooded the wheat fields.* I've never seen a wheat field. No matter what wheat fields are like, I can imagine the flood coming down Mount Lumentza and bending the fig trees, the shacks and the harvests.

The flood has brought something to Isuntza beach. We run there. There is a dolphin stranded in the sand. Flies flutter around its snout and eyes. It has leaden skin, with bumpy scuffs. It has trouble breathing. *I bet you won't dare.* I touch it with the tip of a finger first; then I run my hand over its back. The animal's pungent smell is tattooed onto me. And its pupil is nailed to mine; identical to the pupils of others I'll see agonising in my house many years later.

Gratis et Amore

I go for a walk because Bogdan and Dara have invaded the computer room to go over the translation of their novel and their conversation distracts me. The novel's protagonist is a Bulgarian poet, a prominent expressionist who addressed social issues in his writing and paid a high price for it. The government fined him repeatedly and confiscated his work before he disappeared in 1925, aged thirty. Geo Milev's photo reminds me of the Basque poet Lauaxeta, with his round glasses, starched shirt, and pomaded hair.

Bogdan doesn't really speak to anyone, but he feels the need to mention a fact he thinks might interest me and asks Dara to tell me that Milev's body was found in the sixties in a mass grave near Sofia and was identified only thanks to his glass eye.

That's what they know about me, the title of the book through which I got this writing residency. I say a few polite words and apologise before leaving. I need to get some air before I get into my work later.

I follow the path lined with crab apples that leads to the main road, a gravel track really, and enter the forest after the first bend. There are a lot of leaves on the ground, dotting the grass. I can see a lagoon a little further along; rotting tree trunks break through its green surface, looking like broken bones. Something moves through the garnet spikes of the cattails, a thrush digging through the mud.

I'm nervous: I haven't written anything decent in days. Z. says that there may be stagnant water under or near the house, and this may be affecting my concentration. I have nightmares every night too, probably caused by the spicy food the cook makes for us. Yesterday I told her:

'You're an excellent cook, Rita, but I've been dreaming about men all night.'

Raul, the Chilean journalist, laughs uproariously and requests that she share her recipes with him immediately.

Z. isn't dealing well with my absence, he says. We meet up sometimes to do things we both like: study Romanesque cloisters or the degraded shores of the Nerbioi river, or, equally, discuss the workings of the world sitting in his car in any lost town, holding hands. Sometimes we go into a church and sit down next to each other. I think he prays for me to fall in love before I get tired of our story. I talk to myself and wonder what I'm doing.

I don't want to know how he managed to send me that bouquet of roses. I forbid him from sending me any more presents: all I want is to enjoy his refined verbiage. His rhetoric and lyricism are so from another time that they amuse me. He says I am an oasis in the desert of his existence. Oh, Z., you're my noble troubadour, but I'm afraid you're knocking on the gates of my tower in vain.

Z. says that I don't look after myself, and that's why he had to turn up at that conference, that it was no coincidence. He asks for little, crumbs of my time, and accepts my mood swings and my abruptness with chagrin when I reject his fervour.

He confessed that he'd met me in another life. That he'd been waiting for us to be reunited for so long. He started to cry and I couldn't console him. He will be seventy soon.

He wants to be my chauffeur, my errand boy, my fixer, my nurse, my spiritual guide, my masseur. *Gratis et amore*. This fantasy of his touches me as much as it repels me. His eagerness prevents him from realising that my desires are very different.

I don't dislike the folds on his chin or the scar from his hip replacement. I'm not irritated by his slow pace, or by his habit of complaining about something in every restaurant. I'm not disgusted by his breath, which is sometimes acrid. The way he dresses doesn't embarrass me.

He wants nothing more than to take care of his granddaughter and me. I consent to it. There's nothing wrong with wanting to feel looked after.

The sky looks like a wet flannel. Near the line of the horizon, the earth exhales mauve breath through the bare branches. No noise except the sound of a car, quite far away. The silence is so dense that the clicks on my phone camera as I take pictures sound like the clicks of rifle triggers.

A flock of mallards emerges from the west. Their quacking awakens other sounds in the woods; the call of a magpie, the rapping of a woodpecker. I used to like ducks; I hate them now.

In the park there was a pond surrounded by a romantic railing. One day I noticed that the company of mallards that lived there was spinning round and round one of them as it floated motionless, its head submerged in the water. The blue-headed birds took turns to sit on it. Then they retreated, only to come back again like cats to fishmonger's rubbish bins.

'What's wrong with the duck in the corner?' I asked a man watching the scene. He must have been there for a long time, judging by the number of cigarette butts on the ground.

'She's a girl,' he said. 'They were so rough with her they drowned her. There are lots of males, all those right there are male, but only a couple are females... I don't know where the other one went; she must be shit scared.'

To mate, the male holds the female down by the neck

with his beak. And in this case the gang of assailants hadn't given her enough respite to recover from each assault. The mallards' dull expressions throughout their failed attempts at intercourse disgusted me.

Something cracks behind me. I turn but see nothing. Suddenly I get the impression that the whole forest is cracking, and I'm scared by the possibility of becoming someone's prey. I take out my mobile phone. No reception.

I put my hat back on and decide to return. Fallen leaves creep around pushed by the wind. Someone clears their throat. Pretending nonchalance, I say out loud:

'Good afternoon.'

I'm startled by the echo of my own voice and feel panic attach itself to my insides like a tick to an animal's pelt. I know that the terror is only in my brain, that I'm causing it, and still, an ancestral voice reminds me that there's a price to be paid for walking alone. Nothing is free.

The lights of the big house, on the hill, seem beyond this world. It seems to me that it's infinitely far away.

I start to run, I stumble, I stop. I climb a rock and crouch on all fours, like a cornered she-wolf. The darkness is a walled window, I can't see what's inside. I climb down and lean against a tree. I don't know where to go, I'm lost.

It's really happening now: flashlights, barks, voices. I raise my hands with my palms facing up, just in case.

Three men approach. One of them has a dog on a leash. He is tall and has a goatee held together with a hair band. The other one wears military boots and has very small eyes that make him look like a pig. The third one, a scruffy looking guy, wipes his forehead with a cowboy bandana.

I lie face down. The dog growls beside my ear. They shove the bandana in my mouth, tie my wrists with the dog leash, place a boot on my neck. They will take turns.

The tall man interrupts my imaginings asking me if I'm okay.

'No problem, thanks,' I mutter with difficulty.

'Okay, lady.'

They go.

The moon rises, a crescent moon spreading its light like liquid cement.

I keep walking. I can barely put one foot in front of another: I pissed myself. I lost one of my gloves. A branch scratched my face. I'm soaked in sweat at the bend where the forest and the gravel path converge. Something glints next to the cypresses.

Raised about half a metre from the ground so as not to be eaten up by the vegetation, I distinguish two slabs of veined marble. Tombstones. The same surname, a man and a woman, Mary and Samuel. They may be the former owners of the estate, or perhaps the patrons of the residence. A shadow zigzags across the meadow in front of the house then disappears into the darkness – a deer.

One hundred more steps. I open the door and see Gwen on the rocking chair by the fireplace. She pulls the string and her ball of yarn bounces on the carpet.

'Hello, Miren!'

Knitting is her form of relaxation after a day of battle with her essay collection. Yesterday she happily explained to me that she is turning this garment, which was destined to be a little blanket for her new nephew, into a scarf for her new lover: a change of purpose, a shining example of creative metamorphosis.

'See you later,' I say without stepping into the living room.

I lock myself in my room. I know what I need to say to Z., it's as clear to me as a pattern drawn on wet sand.

And with the sadness of a child relinquishing her favourite

doll, I send him a message. It's short, the epitaph I just read on my walk back. It began on one tombstone and ended on the other, half of it written on one and the other half on the other: *'The Lord gave...' '... and the Lord hath taken away.'*

I lie in bed, unplug the phone, and cry until dawn.

I am awakened by the tinkling of a decorative mobile hanging from the ceiling. As I reach out, I pat the cushions I placed next to me last night, my well-behaved lover.

I go out on the balcony. It is full of dry leaves from the surrounding oaks. The gardener is raking the leaves in front of the house. The traffic noise coming from the road sounds like a harmonica that's out of tune.

Suddenly I notice a hurried trot: there's a squirrel in front of me on an electric cable. I could touch it if I wanted to. It has something in its hands, an acorn.

Squirrels are playful. It may be telling me not to take things so seriously.

They also like to stock up, hide their treasures in hollow branches. Maybe it's suggesting I should start thinking about what I need for my future.

But it drops the acorn. Or did it let it go? How should I interpret that? Release the ballast? Don't accumulate ideas or projects? It's a fact that sometimes the things that squirrels collect are not used by them, but by other animals.

Gwen peeks out her window. The squirrel runs away.

'Aren't you cold?' she asks, throwing a shawl at me, which I catch in the air.

We watch the gardener gather kindling to prepare a bonfire.

'So many branches,' I tell Gwen. 'They look like a pile of bones... I have a feeling that that's what I'm doing too, carrying a bundle of bones from place to place. And I don't mean just the bones in my body.'

'Life is a heavy bundle of bones, darling,' she teases me. 'Haven't you noticed the vultures here these days? They are experts in transporting them. They fly very high and then release them so they'll smash against the rocks... But they don't do that to eat the marrow or the cartilage; they swallow the hard bones themselves, huge pieces sometimes.'

'That takes a tough beak and a tough stomach.'

'Well, don't you swallow them, then. Burn them, like the gardener... And if you are hungry, eat breakfast. Come on, let's head over. What do you prefer with your pancakes, sausages or bacon?'

Daughter of Charity

There were urinals under all the beds. And the sour smell of bodies spread from the rooms to the corridors.

I had chosen my favourite among the oldies. She was a little lady with a hump, her hair bobbed right under her ears and a tortoiseshell hairband always in place. Whenever she saw me her tongue would start moving without a sound; she had been born deaf. I taught her to make the same crafts we made at school and led her to our bench in the garden to get some sunshine.

Flora crocheted little raffia pouches and glasses' cases and sewed my initials on them. Her eyes, when I was with her, changed from sparkling joy to misty melancholy, reflecting back my mood. I think I chose her because she always paid attention: Flora's silence was like a gate that kept out the foolish part of the world, a parenthesis that kept me safe from the voices of routine.

At the back of the hospice was a meadow where we loved to turn round and round with our arms outstretched and our eyes closed, until we became dizzy and fell to the soft ground. Behind windows, old men clapped. Maybe the trampled grass brought back happy memories.

They were sick, disabled, broken in some way; bald women and scarred men, old orphans who'd never known a different roof; people with limitations who encouraged our instinct for kindness and for whom we cared with equal doses of respect and slight repulsion. We started visiting them because the chaplain of the hospice decided to indulge his artistic ambitions by creating a children's choir.

The chaplain was an organist, had a thunderous voice,

and dreamed of winning the Christmas carol contest with his own compositions. Maybe our teachers felt obliged to accept his suggestion, or maybe they hoped that the endeavour would ease the tensions of our incipient puberty. In any case, we lost our recesses to preparing the repertoire.

Since the rehearsals were from eleven to eleven-thirty, we ran from school to the hospice, lined up in the chapel, and tuned our vocal cords to articulate incomprehensible words, neologisms like *ludi* and *txadon* – meaning 'world' or 'church' in a version of our language no one used. Rafaela Arroyo – I think I'm remembering her name correctly – who came from Huelva, in Andalucia, used to say 'Jozu' with a z. It took us a while to realise that Jozu was baby Jesus. Being an *abertzale*, the chaplain had been exiled in the years after the Civil War, and his nationalist ardour demanded such a pure version of Basque that he took it upon himself to resuscitate the most extreme vocabulary.

We got second place in the contest and decided to invest the prize money in big bags of sweets to bring joy to those toothless mouths and hearts scarred by oblivion. Although mandatory rehearsals were over, we kept our commitment to work with the hospice.

Nobody loves the people who live here. That was our assumed general belief.

The rooms in the hospice were spacious, with six or eight iron beds in each. The women's hairdos, badly done chignons, looked like straw scourers, and their bony hands held onto ours as we came to greet them. We were attracted to the hospice: the crutches and canes resting against the pale blue plinths had something heroic, epic, prophetic about them.

There was a first aid kit full of glass jars. Flora and I

would sneak inside to inhale alcohol and other liquids. Those secret raids in which we got high on a diversity of vapours strengthened our union.

There used to be a sleigh-like cart with wheels in the hallway downstairs. Its rider, Tomas, had lost his legs during the war. That weapon was our talisman, the perfect synthesis of danger, courage, and misfortune. However, the veteran Basque Gudari warrior fled from us every time he saw us, turning the cart's wheels with his hands.

'Guardian angels, just what I needed!' he'd mutter.

At the beginning, our families accepted this purportedly civic endeavour, but they worried after a while because spending so much time in the hospice wasn't exactly age-appropriate behaviour. Still, a few of us kept going every Saturday.

One day a man signalled for me to come over. He was wearing green pyjamas and his face looked greenish too, perhaps because he'd shaved badly. His eyes were bulging when he asked me if I knew so-and-so.

'She must be your age.'

'Yes, we're in the same class.'

He started to whimper.

'She's my daughter. I haven't seen her in three years...'

I told him she was good at gymnastics and in the handi-craft classes, and it was true. The man was overcome by emotion, and the other residents got nervous.

'Here we go again!' roared one, dressed in a tiger-print gown. 'Shut up, I swear on Buddha's balls!'

Then a nun came with a tray and asked me to please spend less time with each patient because they got jealous and that, if I wanted to stay, I could help her distribute the afternoon snack, a pink sludge that made you want to vomit just by looking at it.

It was true, my classmate never came to the hospice. According to her, her mother had forbidden it because of all the germs, but T. explained to me that the couple was separated. *The father drinks.* It didn't seem to me a good enough reason to condemn the man to live in such a picturesque mansion. The mother must have been a truly perfidious woman; it was obvious, her very thick eyebrows gave her away.

I was very close to telling my classmate about her father but held off because I wasn't sure I'd be able to handle the consequences.

After some time I saw his death notice in the bakery; I recognised his striking complexion. I wondered if his wife and daughter had attended the funeral and, if they did, did it go some way towards easing the humiliation the man had felt by living in the house where the people nobody loved lived.

A new girl arrived at school in the middle of the school year. We admired her because she was ahead of us in everything. Although she was shy, her skills balanced the saddle of shortcomings that nomadic people inevitably carry with them.

She made oil paintings – she made such a delicate clown for me that my art teacher gave me top marks for it. She was a swift handball player – unlike me, who mainly focused on dodging balls. And she always got the highest marks in the weekly tests – becoming my friendly rival. Her name was the only thing that tarnished her, but we can overcome that stumbling block by assigning her an abbreviation. I'll call her Ana. Ana radiated charisma and intelligence, and instantly inspired in me a deep sense of loyalty.

Back then it was customary to show off a new outfit for Holy Week. We looked like twins: the same plaid skirt, the same high socks with pompoms, the same loafers. And the same yoyo, the same hairpin, the same binders. Twins: she a brunette, and me, a blondie.

'We are more than friends, we are almost sisters,' we said to underscore the degree of our affinity.

We did our homework together, in her house or mine. We went to the tobacconist to buy trading cards. In every visit, Maritxu would paint our nails in the back room and then, even though we were only babies, we'd walk by the boys who were fishing in the quay. Holding hands, we shared the thrill of their whistles.

Our bond was poisoned when my devotion to Ana turned to obsession. I wanted not just the pages where she wrote the lyrics to Mocedades and Serrat's songs to be mine, I wanted her handwriting to be mine too. The summary of her thoughts to be mine only. I wanted Ana to be mine.

'I want to play with the others,' she told me. 'I enjoy playing in a group too.'

My mother often said that it's better to have many friends, not just one, just in case your one friend disappoints you. It was still too early in my life to know that it isn't uncommon for friends to fail – friends we consider unconditional, inconsequential friends or false friends can all fail equally. The reverse of trust is always cruel disappointment.

Resentment rose in my mouth and I regurgitated poison. I burned the clown Ana had painted for me in the bonfire of San Juan and spent the whole summer gossiping about her, telling everyone that her house was full of Spanish flags and that they kept a picture of Franco on top of the TV. She didn't avoid me, but she didn't treat me like she used to.

They moved away the following year because her father was a civil guard, a high commander in fact. She promised she'd write to me. I waited for her letters for a long time, in vain. That disappointment compounded with the previous one helped me learn that arbitrary winds rule the scope of people's affections. For years I told myself that her silence was probably a precautionary measure – she didn't want to give away the lieutenant's posting. I found some consolation in that hypothesis, even though it was stupid.

I resumed my visits to the hospice. Tomas' cart had disappeared on a health inspector's recommendation. He'd claimed that the artefact gave the residence a bad look. I went up to the common room to look for Flora.

There she was, making origami butterflies with newspaper pages. She ignored me when I sat next to her, and I thought that she was taking revenge for my absence in recent months. Determined to break through her aloofness, I pulled out the *Vida y Color* sticker album and a tube of glue and handed her a bunch of trading cards for us to stick together. Flora rubbed her eyes and stood up to leave, as if someone had called her. A nurse took her by the arm then, returned her to her seat, and fastened her to the chair with a leash. Without looking at me, Flora started to draw circles with her index finger on the greasy table, and from that moment onwards nothing was ever the same again.

Inventory of Dreams

Teachers, artists, shopkeepers, housewives, journalists, retirees. Many have shared their anxieties and their deliverances with me. I don't think it frivolous of me to write their dreams here.

One of them told me how she dreamt that she walked out on the street barefoot in the middle of winter. Another, that she entered a glass elevator that went up and up and up and got nowhere. Which of these two situations would I prefer? Running out of resources, or living in an invisible coffin? Maybe the two things are the same.

A young woman told me she used to have little naps in the office during which she saw herself skinning rabbits with a plastic pen. Labour trophies. Afterwards, she'd carry their bloody skins home in her briefcase and hang them out to dry on the balcony.

Another dream sounded like something out of a children's cartoon. This woman I knew saw hundreds of turtles flying together towards the sea, laughing wildly. *We are close! We are close!* She said the dreams started when she separated from her husband and took custody of their children. That surreal scene gave her hope for the future.

A fifth woman confessed to me that she didn't sleep when she got her menses. *My body betrays me*, she said: *when I'm menstruating, an ex-lover sneaks into my dreams, stealthily, like a scorpion, and we fuck*. The dark circles under her eyes were the proof.

The sixth woke up exhausted after spending the night castrating bulls. She claimed to have been a cattle farmer in a previous life and that she owed her skill with scissors to that. *Creating oxen, snip-snip – a true carnage. It must be a form of revenge, right?* I think so.

The seventh described her dream to me as if in a state of mystical hypnosis. *I'm alone and naked and thousands of sparrows appear, and they build a mantle of leaves and flowers for me, surrounding me in a symphony of sounds and smells...* She spoke like this; I used to wonder if she prepared her lines in advance.

However, the most astonishing case is that of the woman who dreams other people's dreams. When she travels, she hears and understands foreign languages. *But how come I was babbling in Italian?* I replied, rather mischievously, that perhaps she'd been touched by the flame of the Holy Spirit. She didn't like it. *The key is the pillow: whoever lays their head on it before me, their sorrows colonise my cerebral cortex.*

And what do I dream of? I have intense dreams sometimes too.

My back ached when I woke up. I'd spent the night curled up and it took a few hours before my muscles relaxed. And my feet ached as if I'd walked for miles.

I have a baby in my arms; my son, I think. I hold a suitcase in my other hand, I'm in the middle of a crowd. We just got off a train and we don't know where to go. Everything feels old, like a black and white movie – the station, the streets, my hat.

I enter a cafe to rest from the weight of my child and my luggage, and walk towards the back, where there is a mirror. I approach and ask the baby: *Who's that, laztana?* Children always answer with a smile; mine, however, clearly pronounces my father's name.

I woke up suddenly. I'd been travelling back and forth to the hospital for three weeks, and found consolation in the thought that I might find some inspiration in the painful situation I found myself in.

I went to the studio to look for a book. I knew it had a purple cover. I'd bought it many years ago because I was attracted to its design. I didn't get a good feeling reading it: the narrative voice seemed cold to me; the narrator seemed a haughty and distant woman who had nothing to do with me. *Une morte très douce*. In that book, Simone de Beauvoir detailed the weeks leading up to her mother's death with a sober, unsentimental prose that I admire today.

I found some underlined sentences.

One: 'In the hallway the doctor said to me: "At dawn she had barely four hours left. I resuscitated her." I didn't dare ask him why.'

Two: 'Astonishment. When my father died, I didn't shed a single tear.'

Three: 'The power of objects is well known: life is baked into them with greater force than into any of life's moments.'

Four: 'When a loved one disappears, we pay for the sin of living with a thousand heart-breaking longings (...) Their death reveals their unique singularity (...) She was just one individual among many. But since we never do everything we can for anyone – even within the debatable limits we set – we are left with many reproaches to punish ourselves with.'

Not even if I'd looked for them on purpose could I have found more accurate sentences with which to summarise my experience, given that thirty years had passed since I'd underlined them.

I prepared to go to the hospital. Another all-nighter in the plastic chair, an invisible demon circling the bed, the disturbing interrupted breath, the moans, the images trapped in my eyelids, my father's command: *I want the band to play Anteron Txamarrotia at my funeral.* And a few lines scribbled in the small hours, while I waited for what was already on its way.

Last night I dreamed of a cat.

It was playing in my room, flicking something snagged in its claw. A lump. *About time!* I say to myself, *Here's hoping you get rid of that rat nest under my bed.*

The cat grabs the trophy in its mouth and leaves it at my feet. When I bend over to pick it up I realise the gift is not a rodent or a ball of dust, but a miniature me, wearing one of my mother's coats. I was an offering to myself, delivered from the jaws of a feline.

I knew I was having a nightmare and wanted to wake up. Impossible: the authenticity of the experience had me trapped. Finally, my own snoring released me from the prison of sleep.

In science hypotheses, experimentation and terminology must be univocal, something that is not true in dreams or literature, fortunately.

Any of those women who had unusual dreams would tell me that they don't know why or how, but that they know fate is about to rattle me.

The Notebook and the Rain

Rain
over the antique market
that is now your life.
– Letitia Ilea

They got me a doll by collecting points from detergent bottles. Since her dress was rather coarse, Amabitxi knitted her a soft cotton jacket and stitched a bow on her hair. I called her Rosalía, a peculiar name that suggests certain classic heroines in the lineage of Matilda, Angelica or Rebekah. She owed her name to a Galician family.

The family – the parents and three children – had come from a village in Ourense and taken over a tavern in the old port. Their regular clients were construction workers and fishermen who came for their *menú del día*. I listened to their mixture of loud talking and abrupt exclamations in amazement, wondering if the commotion was caused by the customers' hunger at mealtimes. I went there every day with their youngest daughter; she took care of me from the time I finished at school until my mother closed the shop. I love to think that as a child I had three fathers: Aita, my father; Aitabitxi, my godfather; and Papá.

Papá ran the bar. I called him Papá like his children did until someone asked him if I was his fourth child. I used the name without realising its meaning: to me 'Papá' was not synonymous with 'Aita', but the name of that affectionate man who fed me cured ham and whose trousers smelled of wine.

Papá would lift me by the waist to sit me on one of the

shelves of the bottle rack. Resembling the bar back cabinets in Westerns, it ran the entire length of the bar and had a tarnished mirror with rust marks and a clock with roman numerals in the middle. The shelf where he sat me was higher than the counter, so I had fun watching things from that vantage point. However, what intrigued me the most was a platform on the ground, under the bar: I don't know what submarine ship or monster I imagined was hiding under the slats. Sometimes I would lie down and peep through hoping to see something, but they would immediately scold me because I'd get sawdust on my uniform.

I also used to play with the radio channels imitating the indecipherable jangle of sounds that emerged when I turned the knob this way and that way. In my mind, I thought I sounded like the foreigners who came to the village in the summers.

From time to time they would make me wipe the tables. I couldn't have helped much, but they had to entertain me somehow.

(It might be worth mentioning at this point that my fascination with the hospitality industry may be a result of this childhood experience. An early poem I wrote goes like this: 'I used to host dreams of tending a bar or tending to the sick / it was all about showing heart, or showing tits.' I suspect the breast-enhancing corsets Estudio Uno actresses wore and the thrill they made me feel contributed to this fantasy.)

Pungent smells emanated from the kitchen, the aromas of meals that were not like ours: Galician *lacón*, turnip soup, octopus with peppers. The water where the octopus had been boiling would remind me of my aunt's lips, which were dark purple because of her heart condition. The mother, who did all the cooking in the tavern, heated my slippers in the charcoal oven.

'I don't know what to call her,' I said, showing her my doll.

'*Pois ponlle Rosalía, que está muy ben, como Rosalía de Castro,*' she said.

Call her Rosalía, which is really nice, like Rosalía de Castro.

'Who is that, a relative of yours?'

I'd said that because I knew they had relatives in Castro Urdiales that they spoke about often.

'*Non, filla, Rosalía era unha escritora da mina terra...*' she'd said with a laugh. *No, daughter, Rosalía was a writer from my motherland.*

And like this, we baptised the doll with a shot of water. Then the mother sat me in her lap – I did the same with Rosalía – and she let herself be overtaken by memories as she cradled us both.

'*Miña terra, miña terra, / terra donde m'eu criei, / hortiña que quero tanto, / figueiriñas que prantei...*'

Soil of mine, soil of mine, / Soil where I was raised, / Small orchard I love so, / Dear fig trees that I planted... When she said those words, which she did often, her eyes would shine like enamel, but when she'd turn to give me a kiss I'd pull away from the icky dampness of her nose.

(It might be worth mentioning at this point that years later, when I came across Rosalía de Castro in one of my textbooks, I was immediately taken by her symmetrical face, her hairstyle, the kindness of her smile and the wide lapels on the jacket of my doll's 'godmother.' I was always drawn to antiques and felt that cameos and ruffled blouses were more 'me' than the two-tone shorts that my contemporaries loved.)

It was in that tavern where the girl I used to be committed her most memorable feat, a milestone that turned out to be a catastrophe, not because anything got destroyed, but because I wrote a story for the first time. To say it like this is to exaggerate a little, but it's not a lie.

The bar boy, their son, used to return on Fridays after spending the week at a Maritime School. He was really nice but didn't pay me much attention. He left his backpack on a shelf in the bar back cabinet and helped Papá serve wine *txikitos*. One day he lost his temper with me and threw a notebook in the air. It was a brown hardcover notebook with cream pages, sewn with thread.

I don't know what I saw in that notebook full of equations, formulas, and diagrams – a miraculous constellation of signs perhaps – and I don't remember when exactly my hand picked up the thick black marker.

I created a whole edifice of straight, curved, broken and spiral lines on the boy's notes, as if an inner impulse were dictating to me to model a knowledge more akin to everything imaginary than to calculus. I think that the embryo of the relationship I would later develop with letters was present in that gesture.

What guided me to draw all those doodles? What was my intention, to write a story perhaps? What story? I have no answers. What I do remember is the disastrous success of my debut.

The boy pushed me and walked away. Papá was angry at the havoc but said nothing. The mum wiped away my tears with her apron and slipped back into the kitchen. Bewildered in that chaos of sullen faces, I curled up next to the umbrella stand. It was raining.

He returned soon, however. And as soon as he saw me in the corner, he gave me a piggyback:

'Irmos, parruliña.'

Let's go, silly. His shoes were drenched, there was no sawdust stuck to them. Ever since then, I've associated clean shoes with forgiveness.

On my next birthday, my family at the bar gave me a notebook with a little key and a lock, a diary.

'Isto é para escribir as túas cousas e non as leas senón ti.'

This is so you can write your things and no one can read them but you. I never wrote anything in that notebook – for fear of spoiling it – but I did on loose sheets, more and more often. To this day, the pull and the risk of blank pages draws me with its power and urgency.

(I wonder if I should mention at this point that a few days ago I stood in the street watching a girl who was about five or six years old. She was looking at some posters intently: the programme for Ea's Poetry Days, a poster for a bike race, advertisements for flats for rent or for sale, and so on. She carried a little folder and was pretending to make a note of things on it, like event organisers do. I locked eyes with her young mother, who shrugged her shoulders and smiled at me.)

Letters to Nadine

Dear Nadine:

There's still an impressionable child inside me who's stunned when someone says, 'No one knows who you are better than I do.' This assertion, excessive as it is, has felt persuasive to me, to the point of even being erotically compelling (this is what someone who wanted to seduce me told me when I was young, and afterwards we went to the cemetery and then I took off my bra).

Do you think I'm crazy? Take what I'll tell you now as a fable.

See: I met a man at a conference. I'll call him Z. He waited for me at the entrance. He invited me to a concert at the Euskalduna Palace; his reason for wanting to invite me being that my voice made him think 'of the sound silk-paper flowers being crumpled.' Can you believe that?

We shall be friends. I'm open to the charm of chocolates and perfume: I'm not made of ice.

It's been too long, Nadine:

I haven't written to you, you're right. For so many reasons:

One. We had a rat infestation in our little garden house. We dealt with it, finally; it wasn't easy.

Two. I'm overwhelmed, with no time for anything. I've been writing reports and samples to apply for a grant for a writing residency.

Z. says he can't be away from me; that I can't go so far away, precisely now that we've been reunited: he confessed in a fit of despair that he believes we met in a previous life.

I can't deny that it's been beneficial to my work to create an invented version of my own life. But I'm bowled over by the fact that someone has inserted me in the invention of their past. Isn't that exciting? Exciting and absurd, it goes without saying.

How are you? And Binoche?

Nadine, *ma belle*:

Z. says that I was the daughter of a wealthy farmer in the highlands of Scotland, or maybe it was Ireland, he doesn't know for sure. I used to wear a corset tied up with leather straps. That I was taller than I am now, and darker. That I was quiet and serious, and since I was always under my mother's watchful eye, I was obedient. I loved learning and liked Latin, astronomy, and philosophy.

When was that? He doesn't know the exact date. He came to us looking for work, and my father took him in. He says he invented a canalisation system to clean the stables by diverting water from a nearby stream. This development was of great benefit for the farm animals and for all the people who lived in the farm.

Our names? He doesn't remember his or mine. A lot of images come to his mind, but no sounds. Let's say I was Mary, and he was Samuel. I lent him books in secret and kept asking him questions about geometry and algebra. He says I did.

He fell in love with me when 'the hills were full of heather the colour of wine-stained lips.' That's how he talks. Isn't that crazy?

He used to wait for me at dusk in the shelter of a copse of cypresses.

He was beaten up once. My mother and I healed his wounds, without saying a word to anyone: we knew my father was responsible for the ordeal. Samuel – now Z. –

had to pack up and leave. It seems I didn't come out to say goodbye.

He became a wanderer. How could he not, being a Jew? But he carried me with him always, like another bone inside of him. More than two hundred years have passed since then.

He says that he knows me like no one else in this world (this assertion must be understood in the context of the transmigration of souls) and that he desires me as much now as he did back then, and that, just like he did before, he accepts my ambiguous feelings for him in this incarnation.

He gave me a fountain pen with a sapphire on its cap, the most expensive gift I've ever been given: 'May the ink flow in synch with your imagination.' Nothing would make him happier than my writing the book I'm working on with it. I am overwhelmed by Z's expectations: he has focused his adoration for me in this one object.

Nadine, *mon amie*:

Incredible news! You searched for the absolute, and you found it! I look forward to meeting this new treasure of yours. However, how do you know that you have found 'your true and final love'? More importantly, does Binoche sleep at his feet?

Z. is sure that I am his forbidden dream because he felt a tingle in his spine when he first saw me: his body told him that I was the one. According to him, this body of mine is the umpteenth incarnation of many others, the current carcass of bone, skin, hair and keratin of those who have been me before me.

You also asked me about the book. What to say... I have to write it, and that's that.

Let me paint you a picture that explains it: you're going

down a river in a raft, not knowing what you're going to find and ready to face whatever comes, whether it be a round pebble in a river's backwater, a heron's feather, a rusty tin can or a sad, wrinkly condom. Writing is about venturing into unfamiliar waters, and dipping the oar – the pen – onward, onward. We writers need to keep going, otherwise the glass oar we carry in our hearts can get stuck in the mud, irretrievably, and shatter.

Nadine, Nadine!

Shocking news: I have a cat! I got him at the start of the year. You have infected me with your softness. I named him Colette. I'll explain why next time.

He's miaowing under my desk right now. I still don't know the meaning of his different miaows. He's uneasy today: animals are like toddlers; they sense our stormy weather fronts.

What's wrong with me, you ask? Everything I'm writing is a big headache.

I can imagine the tut-tutting of my dear departed old folks: 'You're using us however you want in your bloody book, aren't you?'; 'Well, I'll say you definitely have the talent to build a castle out of a single rock!'; 'We weren't the way you make us out to be!'. And whenever this happens I doubt, I hesitate, I wonder... But soon enough, I reaffirm my beliefs: we are all false beings, me above all, we all have multipurpose selves: writers must never adhere to the whole truth.

Other times, however, I imagine them being rather con-descending: 'It's okay, child, we don't mind. You'll hear no complaints from us. You know what you're doing.' I'm not so sure, in fact; I do know I'm sick of it though.

When I was a student I learned that steadfastness is key to progress in any area. When I started working, I learned that it's not unusual to do things correctly only once you've done them badly before. Nowadays, I'd say that perseverance often has a greater impact than talent on results. But the truth is, I'm working on this project without knowing if I'll ever finish it.

Also, O. and I are not at our best. Our relationship is dying.

I will write to you with more details. Be patient.

Nadinette:

I went away for the weekend with Z. Why not. I tried to end things with him when I found the two graves in the woods near the artist's residence 'with our names on them' (!!!). But he is so persistent...

He chose a little country hotel for our escapade, a mid-autumns night's dream. I told everyone I was going on a yoga retreat.

Z.'s skin looks like the bark of a birch tree, and it seems to me that every one of his wrinkles reveals wisdom, experience, gratitude... everything I want for myself. He's an engaging conversationalist, and I find use for everything I learn from him.

Waterfall, birds of prey and us. When we found a stone wall overflowing with blackberries, he said to me: 'I gave you a kiss in a place like this, the only one; that moment, forever suspended, is what held me in the realm of shadows.' You can't imagine how big an effort I made to share this memory of his. But nothing. And what to do. It was too late to step away from the game I'd foolishly entered into.

I saw butterflies, I'm not kidding: we were surrounded by a kaleidoscope of white butterflies. They're harbingers of good fortune. I've given in completely to the signals, I accept them all now.

However, I cringed at dinner: I had a great urge to tell everyone in the hotel that Z. was my relative, nothing more than that – though he is beautiful, inside and out, my dear old man.

He left the curtains in the room open to watch the arrival of dawn. Every five minutes he asked me how I was doing. He didn't touch me all night; I didn't touch him either.

Nadine:

You and I must be among a small number of people in the world who still write letters to one another. Because, really, letters don't ever get lost.

Leaks have caused floods in my flat, not once, but twice. It's been so difficult to turn the catastrophe around. The repairs took forever, just when I was busiest with visits to schools and reading clubs. I had a commission to translate a novel from French, and I needed every hour of the day to meet the deadline.

Just like I did when I was a child, I made lists of words to look up in the dictionary, and passed them on to Z. You can guess how grateful I am that he not only acquiesced to, but became really invested in turning his platonic love into secretarial labour. He is so neat and meticulous, he saved me from having to look up the meanings of that torrent of unknown terms.

Nadine, honey:

O. has left me. He took the lead. Fairground puppet, he leaped out of our movie before my bullet hit him.

He says he needs to spread his wings. He wants to be alone. Onward, then.

Nadine, little sister:

Luckily I reacted. I was trapped in Z.'s delirium, but *c'est fini*: my body and I are more than this flesh my mother brought into the world in 1962. And full stop.

In the end he sent me a message by mistake. I thought he was a widower, I swear. In the message he told his wife that he'd been notified of the appointment for the removal of a melanoma. I had noticed that he never mentioned his wife, but I'd imagined it was out of respect. That's what I'm like, older than my grandmother and more innocent than a babe in arms.

As from tomorrow, I shall not move from my computer: I need an anchor to tether me to earth. But writing is such gradual, dense work... It's exhausting to extract the right anecdote from your brain, to avoid inexact words, to simulate honesty, to maintain your thread between fragments, to add nuance to the atmosphere, to avoid turning depth into banality, to balance the emphasis, keep track of intonation, bind all symbolic elements together, to make sure not to overburden the story with facts or abstractions, and so on.

As André Gide rightly said, good intentions and good feelings are not enough to make good literature.

I'm fed up: all this feels like narcissistic filigree to me.

I must leave you. I need to spend a few hours weeding the garden.

Nadine, *ma soeur*:

I'm not well, no.

The thing with O. turned out to be a bigger setback than expected. Despite our highs and lows, I believed we'd be able to sustain our history through thoughtful gestures on both sides. We didn't have the will for it. *Pax nobiscum*.

We must part ways. It's hard for me to accept. Why? We are like cats: we are obsessed with chasing the sardine that was placed in front of us only because its aroma tickled our noses and we think it's ours. But sometimes we can enjoy the smell without ever taking the fish into our mouths.

O. has left me unmatchable memories (not in the final stretch, though).

One winter afternoon he took me to a pine forest to look at the sea. The full moon, the silver sea... That image has often helped me find serenity. I will always thank him for that. But if I review the decisive moments, I see that he wasn't by my side when I truly needed him. That's who he was: his words were like airborne dandelion seeds.

You need a very muscular arm to put the intimate archetypes of past generations to rest.

How do today's girls manage disappointment? They must have learned something from the women ahead of them. Let us take note of their example: a) hide their despair and b) move on. No more tears; hear the dawn song of new womanhood!

Nadinetxu:

Life sometimes feeds us stale bread: some of us spit it out; others swallow it.

Z. didn't call me, no. He doesn't dare. I don't care: I didn't love him. I miss his pampering though, I'll confess. He hid a lie in the folds of his goody-two-shoes-ness. For fear of losing me, I get it, but what is a lie if not the shield of a coward.

I must admit that, of all the men who have fallen in love with me, this one deserves a double prize: a prize for tenacity (I'm sure that if he were an inventor he'd make miraculous discoveries, given his persistence) and a prize for creativity. He bewitched me with his mirages. The possibility of having lived more than one life has a certain pull... even if you don't remember a thing. Pity that the devotee and the object of its worship were so out of synch though.

This is what I see in the mirror today, after my regular creed turned to dust following this latest setback: a weakened, tired, uglier and disappointed woman. And you know what: I give myself permission to feel useless for a while.

We women of the 20th century have learned to hide the end of love behind a smiling mask. Eventually, this makes it hard for us to recognise our own faces.

Nadinelle:

I'd rather you didn't call me. I don't have the strength to speak.

My brain feels like a gyroscope.

Here's a picture of my cat. I told you I called him Colette, didn't I?

Ça va, Nadine?

The results of my endoscopy and colonoscopy show that I suffer from oesophagitis, duodenitis, hiatus hernia and chronic gastritis. I'm eating healthily, but the irregular schedule I keep is not particularly helpful.

It's not just the stomach: I also feel this scorpion in my lower belly. My doctor thinks that the emotional turmoil has led to intestinal irritation and, in addition to the other medications, she recommended I take activated charcoal supplements.

I feel like throwing up and throw up. I feel like going to the bathroom and go (time and time again I go). I hardly sleep and always wake up with the first ray of light.

Today I went for a walk at five in the morning. I couldn't stand it, there was a rabid dog in my belly... I got to Zorrozaurre; along the Deusto canal, remember? I sat on a bench watching the dredge scrub the bottom of the river to remove dirt and debris. I saw myself reflected in the machine. There was another woman sitting a little further along, and you wouldn't believe what she said to me: 'Your belly hurts too, doesn't it?' She looked like a squirrel.

Ma chère Nadine:

These Carthusian nun habits are good for me.

But life as a cat trapped within four walls is nothing to write home about.

Colette gets bored with me. He comes, he goes, he runs, he jumps on my back and digs his claws... Maybe he's trying to console me: 'While you feel my clawing, the grief won't kill you.' I know that before he falls asleep in his box he will sneak up on me and bite me on the calf and then disappear at full speed, as if to prove to me that he always has the last word. Every day.

No creature is more independent than a cat, they say. I'm becoming more and more of a cat.

Thanks, Nadine.

Yes, I'm better. I've started to sense a hint of something else in the mirror. *La vie est belle,* mademoiselle!

I'm going on a cruise with three friends to celebrate our half-a-century-and-a-bit. We won't be running wild; we are not teenagers.

I hope I don't meet anyone who intends to dictate my body's curriculum.

Hi Nadine!

The cruise? I'm going to write a story about everything that happened. *Mamma mia!*

Did you know that I received a photo from O. on my mobile? It was his foot, with a piece of jewellery caught between his toes: a necklace I'd lost at the beach. He – of all people – found it because it got tangled up in his foot.

I would like to cut out the ludicrous nonsense this type of coincidence awakens, slice it off with the dexterity of the butcher who is about to sacrifice his cattle. But I can't deny it: although I'm not superstitious, I do feel a slight attachment to the mechanisms of magical thinking.

In an interview with Esther Freud, I read something like this: 'One day I realised that things just happen, nothing more; it doesn't mean anything. That was a complete release for me.' My congratulations on being able to break free from the hierophanic interpretation of banal facts.

Now O. wants us to get back together. I thwarted his attempt. How can I risk it? He has his costume too: he thinks he has wings, and fair enough, he might well do. But they are not eagle wings; they belong to another type of flying beast, one that sucks blood.

A hug for you and pets for Binoche.

Lessons

It was like entering a ship, the essence of crushed seaweed filling the nostrils: it smelled of the sea at the butcher's shop.

I used to say good morning to the butcher on my way to school, and he'd respond by raising his carving knife. There wasn't a morning when I didn't pause on the pavement. If he didn't return the greeting because he was busy or distracted, I'd feel vexed: I wanted his cordiality in response to my salute. It felt natural to me.

On rainy days the butcher's wife would lead me into the back of the shop to help her make chorizos. Her hands were always red, stained by the *txorisero* pepper marinade. She'd take the chopped meat from a trough and slowly feed it into the stainless-steel filler after attaching a clean, dry sausage casing to the funnel. I enjoyed watching the raw material become a household staple as the crank was turned.

'Wash your hands... Cut a piece of thread like this... I'll tie the knot... A double knot... Don't handle it so much...'

We hung the strips in the cold cellar and swatted the flies away so they wouldn't lay eggs in the sausages. As soon as she got tired of me, the woman would turn on the radio to listen to a soap opera and send me to her husband with a piece of cotton thread, which, at my request, she'd wrapped around my forearm like a bracelet.

I would sit with the butcher on a bench behind the refrigerator counter. His face was purple, the colour of bacon veins.

'Do you know how to write your name?'

'Yes.'

'Is your teacher good?'

'Yes and no.'

'How is your brother doing with the Franciscans?'

'I don't know.'

'When is Dad coming?'

'Ama knows that.'

There was a sign on the door, a picture of a cow seg-
mented into pieces, each with its corresponding arrow and
identifying name. There was also a blackboard where
products and prices were written in rough handwriting. I
scrutinised those words, spelled them out, the way children
do when they realise that each signifier corresponds to a
signified.

I once grabbed the chalk and added a missing letter in a
word. There were two customers in the establishment. One
of them celebrated my powers of observation; the other
called me *spellchecker*, making it sound like an insult.

A skill that was also a defect.

I have edited a lot in my life, as a teacher, as an editor, as
a writer. I've felt a compulsion to do it: to edit is to complete
something. I still feel that compulsion today: to edit is to
complete myself.

Due to my godmother's ailments, a nurse practitioner often
visited our home. There was silence as the syringes bubbled
in the pot where my grandmother boiled them. They told
me to be silent too, so I'd get under the table with my pots
and play in that hiding place which, according to my imagination, was a hut.

The nurse saw me and asked what I was doing there.

'Making rice.'

'Rice? I don't see anything.'

The balloon of my imagination was punctured, and the
food disappeared instantly from my saucepan.

Reality check.

I have imagined a lot. It's been my way of seeking to give shape to my happiness. I've always been like this: to imagine meant to take possession of something. I still feel that need: to imagine is to take ownership of myself.

My mother was looking at me the way she did when I broke the porcelain coffeepot. On it, a gentleman in a frock coat kissed a lady's hand with a bow. Her powdered curls reminded me of the *rosquillas* street vendors sold during festivals. I don't know what place in my imagination that Rococo painting carried me to, but I used to pick up the coffeepot to look at it, until it fell from my hands.

'Put on your coat.'

Ama closed the shop and I followed her. We didn't hold hands as we walked on the pavement like we usually did.

We rang the doorbell and immediately the Mother Superior led us to a waiting room and asked us to wait there. There was an assortment of prayer cards and a piggy bank on a wicker table. My mother dropped a five-peseta coin in.

Soon the baker arrived with her daughter, who was a bit younger than me. She was carrying a red umbrella, all torn-up with a broken handle and twisted rods.

'Ask for forgiveness,' the hateful nun ordered without further ado.

And since the nuns had taught us that we sometimes committed sins without ever knowing we did, I bowed my head. The other girl looked at me agape. My eyes were full of tears. And then she said it:

'It wasn't her. She didn't break my umbrella.'

Wanting to cheer me up, Ama bought sea snails to eat for dinner. However, having noted how easy it was for the caterpillar of distrust to find soft ground in some people's hearts and for the worm of doubt to find it in others, that event opened a crack in my self-esteem.

To confound and to concede.

I have doubted a lot. Was it beauty or goodness? True or false? Should I go for it or should I give up? An unavoidable exercise: to doubt was to suffer for something. I still have the same attitude: to doubt is to suffer.

And when I suffer, I become the protagonist.

Tenebrae Factae Sunt

I decided to spend the month of November in Wroclaw, but my stay concluded in less than a week. I knew the city because I had lived there for a while when my partner worked for an electrical supply company that sent its employees in deployment to guide the first steps of local workforces elsewhere. Years later I felt the need to revisit the shores of the Odra and all the places I kept in my heart, and I organised a trip with Colette, my cat, as my only companion.

I rented the same apartment in the Czysta building, near the Salt Market Square. In the winter it gets dark before four o'clock in Poland and I knew I would be assaulted by all kinds of nostalgia. But I felt strong enough to put myself to the test.

I was shocked when the taxi driver dropped me off at the building's entrance. The hairdresser and the estate agents under the arcades had closed. Magpies roamed the green areas, rummaging through the rubbish. During the previous visit someone explained to me that scavengers abounded in Poland because the country has seen a lot of wars throughout its history. Scattered here and there were sleeping bags, plastic carriers and blankets. There were no security guards in the building anymore.

I crossed paths with a girl as I entered the hallway. She didn't hold the door to let me through, even though I was carrying a suitcase. I hit her with the cat carrier, accidentally. She cursed at me. She was a striking girl with short hair and a skull tattooed on her neck. I headed for the elevator. It smelled of urine.

Once upstairs I released Colette and, since it was after three o'clock, I went to the market to buy what I needed. Then I called Martin. I was lucky, he'd kept the same number. They still met up every Wednesday at the usual pizzeria. I dressed up and went out.

Martin and the others – young people working in IT and service companies – informed me that they had moved to other neighbourhoods. Rosa and Fermin, a Basque couple from Gasteiz, still lived in Czystan, but further away than before.

'The area has changed completely since squatters moved to the little palace. There's a lot of conflict.'

They were referring to a classical building with extraordinary modernist stained-glass windows. I used to stop on the street to admire them.

'Friday is Independence Day. Last year there was blood in the streets.'

'I'm staying at home this year, just in case. The election is coming up and the right will win, and by a strong margin.'

The city was papered with photos of the candidates.

After dinner, Martin offered to walk me home.

'What are you doing tomorrow?'

'Work until noon and visit the city afterwards. Get to know the places I already know better.'

'Call me if you want a beer.'

'Great... by the way, you don't happen to know what's playing at the Opera, do you?'

'A cycle of choir music, 20th-century composers. It should be good.'

I trusted Martin's judgment. From what I knew of him, he had a talent for combining adventure travel and cultural planning.

'What if we go before the beer?'

Colette kept searching for his place.

'I couldn't leave you at home for a whole month, boy. Don't you want to be with me, silly? You'll get used to it right away.'

I opened the balcony door: I can't stand interruptions to my working day. He sniffed at the empty plant pots and lay in the sun on the plastic table. I went back to my pages. More than once I've burnt my food because I'm so focused on my work, so I didn't realise that Colette had disappeared until lunchtime.

I called him from the balcony. I tossed a slice of ham into the garden, but only an old woman appeared, who shook the dirt off it and swallowed it, winking with pleasure. I pulled his sandbox to the landing in case he might be guided by its smells. Nothing worked. I walked down to the garden, just in case. I stepped on a crushed can and the beer dregs stained my trousers. I felt so uneasy. It tormented me to think that my cat was lost and my throwing him out would be the last thing he'd remember about me. I kept calling. I finally heard a miaow. It came from the bicycle shed.

The girl from the day before was sitting on a tyre, playing with Colette, teasing him with a bit of string. I took my cat in my arms with a rage that took me by surprise, since I'm usually sociable and benevolent. The girl smiled sarcastically and spat on the ground.

The choir first performed a piece by Poulenc based on Paul Éluard's poem *Liberté*, which is a list of places on which the word is written: *On every page read / On all the white sheets / Stone blood paper or ash / I write your name.*

I was struck by the central piece: *Tenebrae factae sunt,* by McMillan. It occurred to me that it could be a good title for a story.

We went to Ela's bookshop afterwards. She was on business in Krakow, so I left a message saying I'd be back, and we stayed for a drink in the square, next to the shop windows. From the Uniwersytet library, groups of students headed to the centre. Their hats brushed lightly against the branches of the willow in front of us.

Despite the guilt I felt at leaving Colette alone, I spent the night with Martin.

The next morning, we had hot chocolate for breakfast and then I went into Saint Isabel's. In Poland, churches are like cash points: people go in and out at any time. Anything you need gets done in an instant – in and out, that's it.

I felt like the city, serenely satisfied in the cradle of Angelus Silesius; I identified with its enigma: 'The rose requires no reason: it blooms because it blooms.'

Colette gave me a warm welcome and didn't leave my side all day.

My mobile rang on Friday afternoon.

'At the Podwale intersection in half an hour?'

When I first met her, Ela had told me that she had travelled around Europe as a young woman and that she still remembered how she partied in a Basque village where they hung geese from their necks during the September fest. I was so surprised to learn that she knew my hometown that I had brought her a plaid blue handkerchief as a gift, the kind worn by sailors and typically by everyone during the festival she'd attended.

They'd blocked traffic. I was incensed to see several swastikas on the stained-glass windows of the mansion. A crowd shouted with their fists raised and the veins in their necks about to burst.

'What are they saying?'

'God, honour and freedom.'

'Let's get out of here.'

'Should we have dinner already? You really liked the pork here, didn't you?'

That evening, apart from sharing our sorrows and our successes, Ela diagnosed me:

'You need an injection of something to write.'

'It wouldn't be the first time.'

We agreed to stay in touch.

I was walking along and thinking how gratifying intermittent friendships are when I heard a hiss behind me. It was her, the girl, with a fat guy carrying a banner. They were about to catch up with me. What were their intentions? Maybe they wanted to steal my bag.

Seeing that there was a police car at a traffic light, I pretended to have gotten lost and stopped to ask them for directions. The other two crossed the road and disappeared.

The journey to the military base was difficult for me. The villages we crossed looked more miserable because of the fog that surrounded them and the unchanging scenery. Rosa and Fermin slept in the back seat. I was beginning to regret accepting Martin's invitation to a day trip.

We made a stop to drink a cup of coffee from our thermos flask in a widening of the road where there was a pile of stacked firewood. A Land Rover drove by and sounded the horn several times. I asked if there was much longer to go. We were close.

Two sectors were distinguishable in the former Soviet base. One of them corresponded to the military units and was surrounded by a wire fence dominated by an anachronistic sign of prohibitions. We made a detour without getting out of the car and then advanced to the other sector, to the dismantled colony.

An immense forest surrounded the whole complex, a

mausoleum of cement, steel, and brick in the middle of nowhere. Gradually the mist rose, and the sunshine made the crowns of the ash trees sparkle.

'I'm not surprised they liked their vodka,' Rosa said.

All the blocks were identical; four floors, each with a little balcony and yellowish walls. One of them was decorated with Slavic motifs. I thought it must have been painted by a woman, a wife who wanted to temper that inhospitable and uniform place with the markings of her people, a mother who saw her offspring grow up in that outpost of her country that was more like a deportation camp.

I took a picture of a bed on the pavement. Rust dripped from it and a small tree was growing through the mattress, a stark image of abandonment.

The houses had no doors and were full of rubble, chipped walls and maps of mould. Something was fluttering with the breeze, a newspaper with Cyrillic writing on it from fifty years ago. My body itched.

We took a tour of the entire village, from end to end: the canteen, the infirmary, the workshops.

There was a dead boar in the playground whose thick fur contrasted with the old multi-coloured court. And on the facade of the gymnasium, graffiti depicted something that might have been an alien foetus.

'We're not alone,' Martin confirmed when he saw a Land Rover parked in front of the building.

We went in and watched them from behind a column.

There were eight: six men and two girls, one of whom I recognised immediately. They were throwing knives at a mannequin, working on their aim. They kept scores. There were bottles and sweet wrappers everywhere.

Martin motioned to us, and we practically sneaked out. We got in the car. We started the engine. There was a soft sound: they'd slashed the tyres.

Then we saw the group come out of the gymnasium. Without thinking, without agreeing, without obeying anyone's orders, we started running towards the forest.

I saw Rosa and Fermin reach a bunker covered in moss. I had a hard time running and I was panting, I'm older than them by a few years. Martin grabbed my hand, and we ran towards some railroad tracks that went over a bridge. The river below looked like a slate of grey cork.

'I'm dizzy.'

'Don't stop!'

We hid in some hedges until we heard the voices of our friends.

Fermin and Rosa chose to walk to the main road and wait for a bus to come by. Martin and I stayed at the base waiting for the insurance tow truck. I told him that I knew the girl, that I'd met her on Wednesday, just as I arrived; that on Thursday she tried to steal Colette; and that on Friday night she followed me with a dodgy-looking man. I felt guilty.

'I'll pay for the wheels.'

He didn't answer. He put on his headphones to let me know that something between us had turned to dust. We arrived in Wroclaw very late. I asked him to stay with me. I got a no for an answer.

I didn't notice the doorbell ringing at first, still stunned by the stress of the previous day. Another ring. I didn't know whether to open the door or not. It might have been the guy from the rental agency, who'd said he'd come by on Monday. He'd come back.

I got dressed to go to the media library to get a video. Some fresh air would do me good. But as soon as I set foot on the landing, I rolled down the stairs. *Tenebrae factae sunt.*

Colette woke me up licking my face with her tongue, my

loyal sandpaper. Blood flowed from my head. Some dirt had made me slip, or some oil or liquid spilled on the stone floor.

The TV and the stereo, my parka and my boots, my mobile phone, my computer were gone from the apartment. My computer. How to explain what that meant?

I put on a hat to protect the cut and barely made it to Martin's office on the penultimate floor of the mall. Everyone stared at me; I was making such a clumsy effort carrying the cat carrier.

He took me to the emergency room and booked me a return flight. Afterwards, he accompanied me to the apartment to pick the rest of my stuff up.

'Write your number down on a piece of paper,' I asked. 'I'll call you with my new number when I get home.'

'No, leave it.'

For the longest time my brain couldn't compute the consequences of that failed episode. I had to start from zero, again. I had gone so far to scribble a few pages, hoping to resolve the enigma of my rose, and the journey had been in vain. Well, no, that isn't exactly true: no journey is ever in vain, even if you don't exactly move forward with it.

The Ashes of Paradise

Plumes of steam rose from the bowels of the landfill. When the sun shone on it, the glinting pieces of metal and plastics gave the mountain of garbage the appearance of a ship. We met there at dusk.

The boys lay on the grassy patches of the lot and waited. We crouched a little further away, among the bushes. As soon as they caught something moving on the hillside, they signalled and fired in unison. Or sometimes they just started to shoot, competing with one another to see who had better aim.

A rat jumped, hit by a pellet, and hid in a nook among the filth only to get out again and run around aimlessly for a while before collapsing, belly up, dead. Sometimes another would move forward a few feet in our direction, baring its teeth, but our boss – let's call him Mikel – demanded that we hold our position.

'We only accept brave girls in this gang.' He said it with such authority that we endured the repulsion the vermin's death rattle provoked in us without complaint: as they lay dying, the rats whined in a way that reminded me of the cries of the patients confined to the hospice.

We'd place them side by side on a piece of cardboard to count them, as if they were fallen soldiers in a war film, and afterwards we set fire to four, six, seven rats. They took a while to burn, and the stench of scorched flesh would stick to our clothes mixed in with the pestilence of the rubbish dump.

One day Mikel brought some lighter fluid to incinerate our catches. They burned instantly, which freed up some time for us to have fun in our fort.

Rats had to be exterminated as they posed a serious threat to the pigeons. They sneaked into the pigeon loft and committed a massacre by eating their eggs. We had built a hatchery for messenger pigeons fifteen minutes away from the village, in Eluntzeta, in a clearing between pines. We named the cock Furia. The bully chased the females.

'Yeah! He leaped on her!' the boys exclaimed as the pigeon mounted a female.

That comment made us want to laugh, but we hid it. Unfortunately, the pigeons were terrified of the rats and barely procreated.

Mikel was the owner of Furia and he too had more than one girlfriend, although I was the main one: he got into the car with me more often. Our kingdom contained the rusty body of a Simca that the ragman had transported with his donkey and cart at our request, in exchange for half a dozen chicks. Our leader hung a sign – PRIVATE – on that rust bucket that we used in pairs or in fours to get off with one another – with our swimsuits on, of course. I liked that pastime more when it rained because our skin gave off mist in the heat of summer. The bad part was that it caused a lot of arguments because we didn't give the others permission to enter the fort until we were well and truly done with our snogging.

Every now and then we welcomed unexpected tenants, disoriented specimens. There was a beautiful female who'd initially fly over the thicket with difficulty, but soon gained strength and was able to fly higher than all the others. The boys called her Greta; we, Gretel. She flew higher and higher, with increasing confidence, drawing wide circles in the air like a pebble in a slingshot, flying farther and farther away.

'Gretel is leaving, she won't be back,' I announced to my people one afternoon.

And she did.

We also adopted a rabbit we found hopping among the rocks; 007. One day we took it to the beach, not knowing that humidity can make these animals sick. It became ill, died and was buried under a eucalyptus tree. We marked the spot with a cross we made out of branches.

We made another cross with a pair of stakes, a perch for a kite. A hunter shot it in the wing and it fell into our territory, a miracle from heaven. Unlike the rabbit, this bird of prey healed on its own. Although, maybe, the fresh rat meat that the boys gave it and the mince we bought cheaply at the butcher's had something to do with it too. I was terrified to bring the raw meatballs to the bird's beak, but I couldn't back down. I had to set an example, being Mikel's girlfriend.

Our hideout also served as a court where we put cowards and disloyal ones to justice. We held Koittadua there for snitching on us and telling the constable that we'd taken a net from a fishing boat's hold. We needed it for our zoo, so we took it. No one punished us, but we applied Old Testament justice to him: we tied him to a bay tree and hit him with bunches of nettles.

We were happy in our hiding place. And we guaranteed the happiness of our animals by doing building work when required. We got the materials we needed from a building site near the school. It was Mikel who opened the lock to the site with a hook. He loaded half a sack of cement on his shoulders, and the rest of us carried as many bricks as we could in the darkness, lighting the way with our torches. We created a pool for a couple of ducks like this, taking advantage of the space between two rocks. The girls would pick up snails to feed them, but from time to time we would also pluck a feather from them to adorn our hair or to use as a bookmark.

We passed cigarettes from hand to hand, and the smoke made us squint like cowboys did as they crossed the Grand Canyon. That mentholated tobacco awakened priceless sensations in us, such as the feeling of having bigger breasts or being great at horse riding. In my case, it made me feel that I could speak French fluently.

Lying on the grass we'd look at the clouds, motionless clusters that reminded us of the coconut slices some of the booths at the fun fair gave out as prizes, and it seemed to us that the weather was still too, way too still.

Sitting next to me, Mikel whispered in my ear. He said he had a surprise in store for my birthday, but I couldn't persuade him to give me the smallest hint.

When the day came, he went to Gernika by bus, with Furia in a shoebox. He offered no explanation; just ordered me to wait in our shelter.

I waited in the blackened ground.

The autumn winds stirred the leaves and made waves in the pond full of dirt. There was nothing left there but the ashes of our paradise: the attack had taken place in September, at the beginning of the school year.

Every year new families came to the village. The men were usually employed in construction and had a reputation for being good workers. I knew a few of the women because they bought stockings in our shop; black knee-highs. The village children and the newcomers usually mingled quite naturally in school. But the last batch was quarrelsome.

They found our lair. They threw stones at us, forcing us out. They plucked our pigeons. They desecrated 007's grave. They took the ducks. They stabbed the seats of our love car. They turned our kite's perch into a scaffold, flying Mikel's underpants from it. They won the war.

That's why we had to make such a difficult decision. And

despite that, when we turned our heads and saw the thick smoke spread through the trees, we smiled proudly.

I waited and waited on the charred earth.

And at last, Furia appeared among the pines. The pigeon landed on my shoulder, and I was stunned to see that it carried a tiny scroll on the washer on one of its legs, a letter with my name on it. And then, I don't know why, maybe because the promise it contained was badly written and full of misspellings, or maybe because the message got stained with soot, I felt really jaded. I walked to the bus station to wait for my boyfriend and, as soon as he arrived, I told him rather bluntly that I intended to go to a different school the following year and he could forget about me.

Soon after that, my first period came, with blood the colour of rotten apples, fresh manure, a muddy toad, a circus canvas, a certain nauseating pink sludge, wet sawdust, a broken umbrella.

Daily Programme

The ship starts moving. The four friends hold on to their hats. They fan each other. Why not feel like a movie star for a week? Who knows what next year will bring.

The dresses flutter in the breeze. Passengers watch the city disappear. Andrea Bocelli sings through the speakers. *Con te partiro.*

Hundreds of terns attend the waterfall of garbage the transatlantic liner elegantly disengages. Waiters with bow ties, loud noise, a tray flying in the air, a pay cut.

The fourth friend remains silent. Why did I even come? Nowhere am I happier than when I'm with my son, my cat, my notebooks, my garden. I feel an anvil in my soul. May God help me.

She retreats to the cabin to vomit. She takes out a notebook. Writes.

Pollution killed the nereids. They no longer attempted to save shipwrecks. Their white robes got old, ragged; they lost their coral crowns. The tridents of hope wandered aimlessly, mixing with the skeletons of the drowned. And now the sea looks like a giant Halloween water park. There is no honey or oil waiting on the shores. The nereids are dead, the constellations are falling apart, the islands are melting. The tear of time shall boil mercilessly on the altars of Carpetworld for all eternity.

She paints her lips in front of a mirror. Her glasses disguise her uneven eye.

They meet in a hall with African décor. Bamboo, tapestries, ivory, masks. The legs of the armchairs are shaped like leopard torsos and dotted with gold freckles. Ladies in sequined dresses and gentlemen in ruffled shirts. Boleros. Cocktails in hands, the sparkle of iridescent fish. To us. Fifty-five. And better than ever, aren't we? Laughter.

They wake up early. There are footsteps on the carpet, murmurs in the adjoining cabin. Through binoculars, they look at a fort to the east, neoclassical buildings, bell towers, palm trees.

The fourth friend doesn't look good. *You don't look good.* My stomach hurts. Fruit salad, eggs, cereals, smoothies. Just a fruit juice? Let's hope it passes. Yes, please cheer up. *Prego.*

Notice. It is forbidden to disembark without authorisation. A flood of tourists on an avenue crowned by a statue of Bonaparte. Market day. God help me.

She buys a stuffed seagull. The toy squeaks like a seabird if you squeeze it. She wears a neckerchief, a souvenir from Ajaccio.

The floor of the chapel, a chessboard. The dome and its filigrees, a baroque cake. The illustrious genealogy engraved in travertine, a weird tree. Someone mentions Louis Lucien Bonaparte and his map of Basque dialects.

Paulina turned into Venus in a canvas. They say that she loved to walk around naked, and she'd have up to three lovers at a time. She died of uterine cancer. Can you believe that her doctor applied leeches to her vulva. *Che paura*! Photos, fans, sweat, ice cubes.

Can you believe that airport bag scanner detected something, and a policeman started examining my toiletries? He must have been looking for drugs. Or hazardous materials. Those worn-out gloves touching my stuff. Sorry. No, I'm sorry, please go on. He even opened the pouch containing medicines: the antacid syrup, the sachets of cystitis medication, the melatonin pills, the Madonna douche gel. He stared at the plastic cannula. Maybe he thought it was an electronic cigarette? I threw everything in the bin. I use it too. The gynaecologist says that there is a slight atrophy on the outer part of my vagina. The nurse looked at me with eyes like a husky. Use it on alternate days. At our age, don't be stingy. You think you're young, and when you least expect it, you realise it's shutting down. Is that why it hurts? I thought it was lack of motivation. It's lack of oestrogen. But what about the atrophy? I had no idea, darling, no idea.

Manoeuvre in Civitavecchia. Exit. They cross, steadfast as the four towers of Forte Michelangelo. Taxi drivers. No, we don't want to go to Rome.

The fourth friend remembers a hotel. Ivy in Trastevere, teeth biting her neck, her head dangling from the edge of the bed, her breasts out of her muslin nightgown. That Rome is far away, and that man, further still. This is not the time for prayers or lamentations. Botticelli never forgot Simonetta Cattaneo either.

They look at the map. The asphalt, melted liquorice. A man watches them from under an awning. He approaches and takes her hand and kisses it. I saw you dancing last night. I'm a musician in the orchestra, Mateo di Lucca. I finish at twelve. *A dopo.*

Such verbiage your pianist, Italian *prosecco.* There you have it, an adventure for your novel. He's a perfect match, even his name! Leave me alone. Sharpen your nails. Leave me alone, please. Let your hair down. God help me.

They are looking for shade. She buys cologne in a shop. T. slaps her. Who is it for? For my son. I'm not sure I believe you. You must leave the past behind. Should we go back and take a dip in the pool?

Daily Programme, night party. White clothes, white bags, white jewellery, white sandals. Hundreds of fools rehearsing a ridiculous choreography. Twelve o'clock and a hand on the waist. How did you find me? The colour of your hair, *cara*.

They walk down the steps. They get into the water, away from the commotion of children. Oily puddles, the iridescent sheen of sun lotions. A stab in the foot. *Niente.*

The fourth friend swims in Porto Venere. Wide strokes, the bombastic gestures of an orchestra conductor. Thank God the bikini covers my stretch marks.

Matteo dives in and brings out bright things. Sea glass, pieces of mother-of-pearl, pull rings, shells. Matteo tells her where to look. *Quella grotta*, Lord Byron. *That cave.* God help me.

She feels her tiredness in the sway of the algae, in the stillness of the rock, in the invisible saltpetre, in those clouds that look like locks of hair. What if something happened to me? Percy Shelley drowned near here. What a nightmare for poor Mary!

What is he holding in his arms? Tentacles, siphon, suction cups, eyespot. The octopus' head is soft, like the skin of the penis. *I'm here, touch me.* He touches her jaw, shoulders, buttocks, lips. Matteo's hands part her thighs. This has nothing to do with my loneliness. It's as logical as a crab eating a shrimp. A white string floats in the water, strange ink, a stream of toothpaste, a string of béchamel sauce. *Wait for me today.*

Genoa is shaped like an amphitheatre.

At ten o'clock, a visit to the cemetery. I like necropolises. We're going to tour the city, *piano-piano*. Aren't you going to tell us anything about yesterday? I spent the whole day in a bubble. Forty-three. No, he doesn't have a wife.

The fourth friend struggles with her reasoning. The artery,

the ligature, the nerve, the fibre – are so slippery. It's hard to intertwine concepts. That's why she loves cemeteries: the dead don't give a shit about the doubts of the living.

The configuration of eternal rest through neat little gardens. Angels, arches, fountains, capitals. The sun lighting up tombstones as if following a code. Something falls from a tree. A card. A tarot card? How is that possible? Tell me it's not The Star. No, it's The Fool. A good sign. Matteo kisses the card and places it in her cleavage. *Salvalo li*. God help me.

A lump in the middle of a passageway under cedar trees. A dirty cat trembling in the heat. There is nothing to do. Please don't let anything happen to Colette. A string quartet plays Paganini.

She waits, sitting on a stool. Cleaning staff, buckets, hoses, rags.

The sea. A merchant's blue velvet. In one of Yourcenar's stories, seven merchants travelled to *terra incognita* in search of sapphires. The jewels liquefied, melted, fell apart, disappeared. Those who seek the absolute must get used to coming up empty-handed.

Give me your hand. In your dreams, this is not the *Titanic*.

The moon. Clock without hands, holy host, the eye of the Cyclops, the tunnel to Neverland. In a Méliès film, the moon had a face like a cookie. A cannon fired a rocket. The rocket pierced one of the eyes of the moon. I will never hurt you. *Io non ti farò mai male.* Words, *bambino*, words, *parole*.

The wake of the ship, a pastry of oil and silver. She hooks up her skirt as she approaches a speedboat. Will the moon be the same after Genoa? *Chissá.*

Our summer night's dream is over, *ragazze*, our *sogno di una notte di mezza estate*. Such a pity. Life does sometimes look like a summer night's dream, doesn't it? Yes, if you navigate with the coordinates of good fortune. Laughter, cackling, joy, guffaws – hens disembarking the henhouse.

The fourth friend takes The Fool out of her pocket. She tears it up and throws it in the water. She has learned to ignore sad eyes, music in the veins, frugal loves and full moons. It's healthy to play with hooks only if you're not going to get hooked. Coin a farewell formula. *No più giocare alla roulette russa.* I don't want to play Russian roulette.

When she gets home, her cat stares at her first. Afterwards, the stuffed Corsican seagull.

Her son hugs her. Italian cologne! Thank you very much, Ama. The fragrance is a bit strong... but it doesn't matter.

She unpacks, loads the washing machine, checks her mail, hangs her clothes to dry. She takes a shower and what's new pussycat, butterfly, tadpole, starfish, jellyfish? Where is my notebook? And she leaves the notebook on her desk. God help me.

Yesterday's Girl

Memory is something like a place where we once lived. Random summaries of the past are always set in concrete settings, even if the framing is somewhat blurry.

D., my best friend from high school, gets pregnant at seventeen. I go to the wedding by bus on a Saturday in April.

I wear a hippy blouse with copper stitching, jeans, and bobbed hair.

My left eye is deformed; I haven't had a single operation on it yet. In a photo I cover it with my hand, I don't know if intentionally or by chance.

Most of the girls wear electric blue, which was fashionable that spring. With their hairstyles, jewellery and boutique accessories, they don't look like teenagers, but executives.

One of those girls was found dead in a field on the outskirts of Barakaldo. She was doused with gasoline and killed, not long after high school. The specifics, the motive for the crime, were never resolved. I don't remember her name and surname right now.

D. was wearing too much make up and a wide smile. Her mother was a widow who made a living cleaning cafeterias.

'I'll keep attending class until the baby is born,' D. told me after slicing the cake and gifting me a box of matches with the wedding date engraved in gold.

I hardly knew her boyfriend. D. didn't really know him either.

He was older than her. He worked in a factory. They sent him to jail shortly after the baby was born.

One day I went to visit my friend. A woman came by to

let her know that relatives of political prisoners held support meetings regularly and she was invited.

D. found work at a fishmonger's and dropped out of school.

'He was freed without charge,' she let me know on the phone after a while. 'They've stolen two years from us, the bastards, but we have our whole lives ahead of us.'

'Memory preserves its old rhetoric, it rises like a tree or a Doric column; it usually sleeps inside our dreams and secretly we are its exclusive owners', Silvina Ocampo wrote.

On Mondays, girls would share their weekend adventures in the playground.

One confessed that she'd stained her underwear green on a field in the back of a disco. Another that she had danced very close with so-and-so and that at the last minute she'd let him put his fingers inside her.

We imagined things differently: that when we met Him – like Amanda did on the wet street in Víctor Jara's song – our souls would merge into one and ascend together for all eternity in an unsurpassable epiphany. And so, hope encouraged us to be patient, whispered that we would find true love in the sweet shop, at a summer festival, any day, anywhere.

That doesn't mean we didn't have blood in our veins. At night, in bed, I would mentally review film clips. The first is a very early one from *Topaz*. The protagonists are standing in the semi-darkness. The guy lowers the strap of the girl's slip (incidentally, that strap trick has worked wonders in my sexual experiences). Another scene that perturbed me, making me feel as if pepper-smeared horsehair was being rubbed against my skin, came from a really bad film where Dr. Victor Frankenstein seduced a servant girl and brusquely ripped the ribbons of her gown.

Such were the torrid fictions that I transferred from the big screen to my own imaginings.

Although we did not possess stories of our own, we were still part of the club of confidantes of the savvy girls. I enjoyed the approval of D.'s circle because almost no one else did Latin and Greek, and because my class notes for other subjects circulated quite successfully among them.

Back then, I considered Rousseau, in his powdered wig, the basis of every intellectual paradigm. *Discourse on the Origin and Basis of Inequality Among Men.* So misogynistic, and such a scoundrel, handsome Jean-Jacques – and yet, there I was writing a synopsis with multi-coloured BIC pens.

'Akelarre is playing in Deba this Saturday. Are you up for it?' The girls who treated the calendar as an orange teased us. 'And next month, Egan plays in Markina.'

No witnesses can verify whether something happened this way or that way. And the memories we keep are always partial in any case.

In adolescence everything that wasn't shocking was natural, like the mist that encircled Ondarroa throughout the school year. Because we used to arrive at the institute before the janitor opened the gate, we would take a walk in the boulevard, bundled up in our tabards. We did not wear white scarves, like the protagonist of the most romantic song of the time, nor did we have Levi's jeans, suede coats or riding boots, like the daughters of ship builders, but jeans of indifferent brands and Gorilla boots. We saw those girls in the bar smoking cigarettes with a tortilla *pintxo* on the side. We, devout readers of Martín Vigil, said *vade retro* to all temptations.

The huge breakwater made it difficult to see the sea.

Gran Sol was many miles away, but by then I no longer cared: my father had switched to merchant ships and was on the Durban-Rotterdam route after many years on trawlers. He and the boss had quarrelled due to a series of engine breakdowns that Aita had not been able to solve. They had to return to port several times, interrupting the catch. They argued. My father, angry because he couldn't find the cause of the technical problem, left the company without even collecting his settlement. Weeks later, an acquaintance found him a job in a shipping company, and Ama and I got into the habit of writing him letters and sending him photos.

The strike of the previous year had hit the coast. It started after Christmas with the support of the entire fleet. It was a tough strike. For three months my father came home late because he was a member of the bargaining committee. My mother reluctantly admitted he had a responsibility, but was afraid of retaliation.

The mooring of all ships caused shortages for the canneries, transport and workshops that made their living from port activity. They created a resistance box. They organised donation rounds to raise funds. Some decided to look for work on land.

We also saw more than one family – Rafaela Arroyo's, among others – return to their places of origin with all their belongings in tow. I had the feeling that they left pieces of broken roots behind, in all corners of the town, invisible remains that no one would pick up.

We forget the details. However, from time to time – whether by coincidence, statistics, or the summons to a demonstration – ghosts that slept in our inner sanctum awaken, both the disgusting and the radiant ones.

In this environment of sizzling hormones and social protests, we collected stickers. Our beaks were already breaking through the shell, but our demands were not related to the strikes of the fishermen or those of adjunct teachers; our demands were of a different sort: we wanted a bus service to go to Venice – a disco – on Saturdays.

We hitchhiked, our lips super shiny with Margaret Astor's lip-gloss. Besides passing all exams with flying colours, our main objective was to catch emotions in that dive club above Saturraran beach and have stories to tell, at least to ourselves. This desire filled us with guilt, since the core ingredient of our education was obedience. Our mothers carefully instilled in us the moral compass of their generation: modesty and compunction.

One afternoon two older boys stopped to give us a lift. Without warning, they stopped at Milloi Peak and went out to piss. We saw them from behind in the darkness, lit up by the headlights: legs apart, little jerks, the gesture of zipping up. After that one of them climbed into the back-seat, grabbed T. by her waist, and started kissing her on the neck. We started screaming. The boy backed away in shock.

'Start the car,' he told the other. 'These ones are way too green.'

We forget the arguments. However, sometimes someone else's memory resuscitates, with complexity and modesty, the person we used to be. And the people who used to be with us.

The literature teacher read aloud to us from *The World According to Garp*. I can still see him sitting on a desk: with his moustache, two overlapping shirts on, and his scruffy trainers. His teaching was an eclectic mix. He discarded the curriculum and brought us his own books in packing boxes so that each of us could choose whatever we felt like and then work on it according to his individually-tailored criteria.

What was the world like according to us? That remained to be seen. I used to make up stories for D.'s future baby on tracing paper.

The P.E. teacher made us run from the mudflats of Zaldupe to the Cofradía Vieja. He timed us. His eyes went to our chests, to the nipples the cold tattooed under our cotton T-shirts. Our misty breaths formed another whitish path parallel to the river scum. This was our athletics track, a path along the banks of the Artibai.

I would be at the tail of the platoon, wheezing. Since D. was exempt, she would wait for me in the library with puffy lips and her borrowed beige maternity dress.

The Latin teacher with her Pantocrator face gave us hell, relentlessly. The quotes she had us translate were taunts meant to hit us squarely in our souls. *Ut sementem feceris, ite metes.* You reap what you sow. *Vitam regit fortuna, non sapientia.* Life is luck, not wisdom.

D. smiled all the time imagining the face of her son, her daughter. Ultrasounds didn't exist back then. I had a feeling that we would drift away after the delivery.

'*Amor omnia vincit,*' she consoled me.

Some memories replace others. Weren't the first ones consolidated in memory? Why is memory not a neat, rich and reliable store?

As soon as I enrolled for my degree, I started dating a boy I had met at the wedding. S. was five years older than me, and he drove me to my rental apartment near Bilbao in his space blue Citroën every Sunday.

I didn't bleed. I didn't bleed, neither the first time nor at any other time. I don't know when my hymen tore.

Maybe it happened on some occasion that my hippocampus has erased. We did it for the first time between a Formica table and a brown plastic armchair, on the parquet floor. He loved me; I loved how he used my body.

I spent hours in that apartment where the psycho-pedagogy syllabus and the new Basque novel became walnut shells that transported me far away, slowly but surely. But he had plans: as soon as I graduated, we would go to Dijon. I was fluent in French and would find work as a teacher or in a kindergarten. He would do maintenance work in a hotel; his brother could recommend him. We would live with his brother and his wife. He made my hair stand on end even before going into the details: I had zero longing to become an immigrant. And besides, S. smoked cigars, and always asked for coffee and a boozy shot for dessert, like lorry drivers do. I was not ready to accept the whole package.

At dusk, I would turn up the collar of my raincoat and pretend to be part of a seductive narrative: I was Maggie too, the one in the story, and the cranes and shipping con-tainers in Uribitarte were those on the New York docks; and the minibuses, the train station and the neighbourhood around the medieval bridge were really Hamburg. The aes-thetic package of city sensations and its melancholic inhabit-ants made up a universe that fired me up.

One day S. accompanied me to our storage space – the place that had once been my mother's shop – to look for a backpack that I needed to go hiking in the Isaba mountain range with my university friends. He was angered by my stinginess: he wanted me more passionate, more devoted to him. He grabbed me by the neck and pretended to strangle me, half-seriously, half-jokingly. I wasn't daunted, although I was trembling. He stormed off. I got a bruise on my neck from the squeeze; it looked like a love bite. I didn't dare tell anyone what had happened.

What words could I use to leave S.?

'Now that you no longer need a taxi driver, of course. You whore.'

But he kept coming back. He would park under my house and stay in the car until dawn. My mother wouldn't even let me look through the shutters. A few half Valium helped me get through it.

In the following months the gossip got back to me. I had split him in two, destroyed him; I was the guillotine's edge, I was soulless. He made me out to be the reason for a string of unfortunate events. It's true that he went through some misfortunes, from what I heard.

I saw him not long ago near the Alderdi Eder carousel, in the gardens of Donostia. Still as attractive as ever, even though almost forty years had passed. He was with a woman taking care of some children, perhaps his grandchildren. I went to say hello, it didn't cross my mind not to.

'In the end you got what you wanted,' he said.

I sensed an ancient resentment in his tone, the breath of powerless, useless, null affection.

'And what did I want?'

'To live your life.'

Oblivion is an adaptive reflex of our mind. A necessary mechanism to avoid overwhelming the grey matter.

I was recently approached by a couple with their two children at the end of a recital.

'Have I changed that much?' the woman asked me.

Singular trees, no matter how old, never lose their bearing: I recognised D. from her smile.

We did a quick summary of our biographies over wine, reviewing the most relevant events in our chronological friezes.

'Do you remember our song?' The French teacher used to put it on the cassette player. 'It was about a young postman...'

'*Le facteur*. Of course I do! It was by Moustaki, and quite corny, but we were so corny... The postman was dying, and lovers' letters didn't reach their destinations...'

'It was good enough for us to get a general sense of things... I remember one day the teacher asked the meaning of a particular word. And you said quietly, but we all heard you: "nightingale".'

'Really?'

'We were speechless. It was magical.'

It was magical.

Tomorrow I have a meeting with students at the school in the town where D. lives. I plan to go to her fishmonger's. She will take off her scaly gloves to hug me.

'Let me treat you to a meal,' I will tell her.

'If you don't mind waiting an hour...'

We have all the time in the world.

If we neglected to meet, we would both lose a chunk of the hypothetical future of the friends we used to be: what's possible will not return unless we give ourselves a chance. I wouldn't like to find out one day through a common acquaintance that D. died of cancer, or for someone to tell her that I died in an accident. It is not yet too late to cross the dividing line between the lived and the unlived.

Memory is a private space, but not a small one. And fortunately, it's roomier than the basket of oblivion.

Intermittent Journal

To look for the literature in each and every story, to think of tone,
To feel the tone. A situation, a note, a passage.
– Esmeralda Berbel

Miramar, March 2013. To write trees. As a child I drew trees. I put a nest with two birds in all of them, both birds with open beaks. Although they were more sketches than proper drawings, they made me feel good. That feeling grew when it occurred to me to draw fruits on the branches.

I placed a pear, an apple, a banana, a pair of cherries, a fig, an orange, a lemon, a pineapple and even a tiny strawberry on the branches, the sum of the fruits I knew.

I believe that the splendour of those absurd trees lay in their abundance: they inspired safety and enjoyment, although I did not rationalise it that way at the time. Be that as it may, I was immediately aware that my hand, through each stroke, had the ability to turn certain desires into metaphors: my ramblings were reflected in those sketches. The child, like the adult, is capable of synthesising abstractions into a squiggle.

Didn't I come across impasses and empty spaces in those drawings like the dead ends I encounter today when I write? I must have.

This eagerness to analyse my life encourages me to summon the past and the present, locking them into the same axis – the book I'm writing – to find parallels. Even though their points of convergence emerge from intuition and the imagination of memory, more than real experience or logic.

Krakow, November 2014. Pages under pebbles. On the edge of the Jewish Quarter there is a synagogue with a cemetery on one side. It looks like an abandoned meadow. The insistent drizzle has clouded our good cheer.

There were little piles of stones on most of the graves. What do they represent? The number of visits? Or the sum of the promises kept? Are they randomly chosen stones? Or were they lovingly brought in from a specific place?

Stones, the permanence of memory.

There were pieces of paper under the stones too; notes, maybe, or letters. Respect made me hold my hand back and not pry. There were folded newspaper pages as well, long-awaited news perhaps.

There were no flower bouquets. Only stone on stone, and on paper.

Bera, Bidasoa, August 2018. My friends' garden. A couple is hosting me at their home in Bera, in Xantelenea. It has a large masonry portal, with the number 7 carved on the lintel. On the ground floor they keep a hand-carved grandfather clock, a trunk and deer antlers. Their grandparents' bakery's workroom used to be here, they tell me. One of the rooms upstairs has a marble fireplace and an antique desk in the corner.

The rear part overlooks the garden, where hydrangea beds abound. In the centre stands a dense *albizia julibrissin*. This variety owes its name to the Italian naturalist Albizzi, who brought the plant from Constantinople in the 18th century. It is better known as the 'Persian silk tree'. Its flowers look like tulle pompoms. There are also fir trees, one of which was planted by my friend when he was a boy. Its size confirmed the beneficial effects of time to me.

We can hear the Xantel river.

Under a canopy of wisteria, a stone bench. *Aunt Carmen*

used to write there. I imagine a young girl who kept to herself to compose verses. *She wrote a trilogy,* Uphill and Downhill. *One of her novels is called* Impatience. A good title for my situation.

At night I had a terrible dream.

I was in a casino. Upon entering, I checked my coat into the cloakroom, but they wouldn't return it to me on my way out. I've never been to a casino. And yet, my subconscious reveals the outcome of my last bet with absolute clarity.

I walk into the garden early, with a glass of water, a cushion and my notebook. Blackbirds among the hibiscus flowers.

End of the weekend. My hosts send me off with a sheaf of hydrangea cuttings to plant in Miramar. Sharing plants means spreading the location of our desires.

Paris, Musée d'Orsay, December 2015. Harvesting the void. I look at Millet's *The Gleaners.* Three women collect wheat spikes leftover on the threshing floor. The little they carry on their aprons contrasts with the evident abundance behind the fields.

The other day a friend told me that whenever she's going through a bad patch, that painting assaults her senses: she sees herself in a field from which the harvest has already been taken. But she is still looking for something; she searches for loose grains. The wind takes what she has gathered from her hands. She knows her basket will be empty.

Perhaps because I am from the coast, I usually see myself submerged in water, broken shells digging into my feet. The gale arrives and sand hits me in the face. I can't open my eyes or move.

Do we know what to do when our world shakes? Resist and wait. Resist and wait. And have hope. Or is that a different exercise?

Chicago, January 2016. Bestiary. Ants roam the edge of the bathtub, excited by the scent of body lotions. Rust-coloured ivy clings to the window and vibrates every time a train goes by. A kimono behind the door. I wonder if Gwen wears it when she brings a lover home.

The rub of the spandex in my bra has caused sores under my breasts. This is what travelling entails: swollen ankles, occasional constipation, sleep disturbances, physical discomfort that the change in scenery usually compensates for.

During the meal I notice details in the apartment. Happy photos, a thirst to experience every moment with intensity; Gwen likes to give two fingers to adversity.

On a shelf on the dividing wall there are several animal figurines: a flamingo, a whale, a ram, an Arabian camel, a grasshopper. *My totems.* Totems? *We are a little old to believe in such things, aren't we?*

Rachel is here for coffee. She works as a cleaner, which allows her to rent a garage where she teaches dance classes. She tells us that she plans to cross the country on a motorcycle. She has the features of an angel in a Russian icon and even the way she talks is angelic. She explains the reason for her decision as if it were a miracle: *Tonight I dreamed that I roamed the seas on the back of a dolphin.*

Alphonse and Carlo turn up too. The first works as a driver; that's how he earns the money that art doesn't pay and can afford his mother's stay in a mental institution in the outskirts of Tours. A crow that slammed into his window, breaking the glass, changed his fate and made him decide to leave. *I had to do it: it was either my mother or me.*

The other one plays a piece on the piano. He is a spinning instructor during the week and prefers jazz clubs to his family's network of pharmacies. *In Ferrara, every time I lifted the lid of my piano, I found an insect on the keys. I would have rotted there if I hadn't moved.*

The atmosphere is good in the neighbourhood. Beauty centres, bars, art galleries. Gwen and I sat in a park. Suddenly, something falls from a poplar and rests on her forehead. A ladybird! *Your third eye just popped out,* I tell her, joking.

We go to a bazaar. I wait for her while I observe a neon ad, sex services. It doesn't take long for her to come out with one more figurine for her altar. It's red, with black spots. *I want someone like me by my side.*

Our creeds are made up of our statements. And our recycled creeds are our propulsion engines.

Miramar, Valencia, May 2018. About eagles and parrots. We shortcut through the orange grove to the village. The light in this region is good for me. A week at M. J. E.'s house; a cure of friendship.

I am plucking my own feathers, I confess to her. And I tell her a story that O. used to tell. He used to tell it with fervour; it'd get him all fired up.

There is a very long-lived species of eagle that owes its longevity to a feat it performs when it starts to feel old. When it notices that its claws have lost flexibility and its beak has become so twisted that it risks piercing its chest, the eagle is faced with two options: welcome death or be reborn. If it opts for the latter, the eagle takes refuge in an abyss and hits a rock wall until the beak falls off. After a period, a new beak sprouts through, which it uses to pluck its claw nails. And as soon as the new nails come out, the eagle plucks out its old feathers. After five months of torture, the eagle flies triumphantly to live on for thirty more years.

It's a myth, not biology: it's impossible for any bird to live that long without food.

That's where I'm at, removing everything that doesn't do me good from my life, I tell my friend. She takes my arm. *Well, be careful, you don't want what happened to Camila, our parrot, to happen to you, you know. She went mad with grief. She began to peck and pluck her feathers with such fury that one morning we found her dead in the living room; she had bled to death.*

When I mention the title of the book I am writing, M. J. E. pulls Montale's *Cuttlefish Bones* off a shelf. It's neat, not a throwaway word in it, everything is alive. I leaf through it and I'm left with two premises: first, don't mix the essential and the transitory; and then, this sentence: 'Not the cricket but cat / of the hearth / now he advises you...'

Miramar, June 2017. I have never been so alone. I take my shoes off. The grass pricks my feet, just like the obsessions that plague us no matter how hard we try to get rid of them. I no longer have a San Juan bloom, that shrub my godfather planted.

I've come to burn a piece of paper. One more rite.

I claim to my desire to grow and overcome on that page. Artaud said: 'Burn the papers!' A laughable comparison.

Today there will be no bonfire. Before, it used to be O. who'd oversee lighting the fire while the rest of us prepared dinner. If we got tipsy on the wine, we danced around the fire without music. Such a nice gang. When the others left, we made love in the little house, standing against the armoire.

San Juan bagilean, denpora ederrean, arto eta garixek gorde,

gorde; subeak eta zapoak erre, erre. San Juan dabil oin-puntetan, solo guztixek bedeinketan...

Saint John's in June, beautiful weather, corn and wheat, keep them, keep them; toads and snakes, burn them, burn them. Saint John walking on tiptoe, Saint John blessing the orchards.

If only the bonfire would burn away not only real snakes, toads and weasels, but also all the metaphorical predators... Was there ever (will there ever) be a time when I didn't (I won't) need ritual purifications?

The pile of kindling awaits.

We must go through this ritual burning from time to time, mindful of the wind so that what's beneficial doesn't turn against us. The rotten fruit, the nettles, the dry leaves will feed the bonfire in its slow work of destruction. Sometimes the flames are not visible even though the pyre is lit. The smoke, light or thick, will always disperse, yet the smell lingers. And despite the fact that its fortune is precisely to get lost – so many ellipses, so many episodes deleted on purpose, so many reasons to leave this or that aside – the ashes will remain on the earth, to be used again.

Burning, breaking, burning. Just as a pond is a body of still and sleeping water, this pile is also made up of patient materials that appear to be asleep.

I burn the piece of paper with a match. The mini bonfire didn't help me to relax. I change my mobile's wallpaper to a photo of a sculpture that captivated me in the Lviv cemetery.

Bilbo, September 2013. L'étoile. A woman squatting at the edge of a spring, naked. She holds a vessel in each hand, but she doesn't collect water; instead, she pours it into the fountain. One of the waters is clear and the other is dark.

Suppose that one of the waters is the past and the other is the present. The two waters mix in the stream.

Suppose that water is writing, since the woman has two mouths: one on her face, as is usual, and the other on her belly, under her navel.

Behind the naked two-mouthed woman is a tree.

Suppose that it's the Tree of Life, since its canopy is round and its roots are visible. *The tree that opens all doors and heals all wounds,* as Montgomery Clift said in *Raintree County*.

There is a large bird at the top of the tree.

Suppose that bird is death.

The sky is crowded with stars.

This image is a card from the 17th-century Tarot de Marseille deck, The Star. I found it yesterday right next to the fountain in Doña Casilda Park, in Bilbo. Did the wind bring it? Did someone leave it?

I've kept it so I don't forget what I'm doing.

Ezkaba-Urepel, July 2018. A pentagram in the forest. When we reached Errotariborda, the miller's hut, we hugged trees.

The beech is rough against my cheek. I would like to speak to the trunk with my hands. If this trunk were the trunk of a man.

My belly hurts.

We resumed our march. We are five women, a somewhat dislocated pentagram. The notes are our comments, a cough, our laboured breaths, a song, our complaints. The key, our itinerary.

I see a feather on the edge of the path. It is enough for me to know that it's reddish.

Paris, Père Lachaise, December 2015. *Ici repose Colette.* This place looks more like a park than a cemetery. How many bones are there in seventy thousand graves?

Apollinaire. Modigliani. Camille Corot. Gerda Taro. Miguel Angel Asturias. Edith Piaf. Max Ernst. Chopin. Gertrude Stein. Consuelo Suncín. Sophie Germain. Balzac. Rossini. Tell me: do your ghosts hold orgies when the bell rings at midnight?

Voilà. It's simple, pink granite. The inscription, without artifice: *Ici repose Colette. 1873-1954.* That's it.

I review a quotation from her *Journal Intermittent*: 'I used to tell myself that what remains materially is insignificant and that the dead have nothing to do with the living. They are only resurrected in a memory, in an image, in the unforgettable sound of a voice, in meticulous writing... in the hours of tender adoration and despair.'

I resuscitate my dead more and more often.

When she was a child living in the Bourgogne, Gabrielle Sidonie Colette would get up every morning at dawn and walk through the forest to reach a fountain and drink water. It is said that she rejected all tragic perspectives on life. And that she learned not to gamble everything on the roulette. She made a commitment to her strength.

An old woman approaches. She opens a few tins on the grave and starts distributing food to a gang of cats with a teaspoon. *Madame, did you know Colette?* If she did, she must have been quite young at the time. The lady tucks a pair of rollers under her wrinkled handkerchief. *Mais non! But is there a better place to pamper these sacred beings?*

Wroclaw, February 2014. Jesters and gnomes. I have rediscovered Szymborska. Her ability to combine scepticism and paradoxes is admirable. And so surprising, her ability to place herself in other realities – be it a grain of sand, a star or a beetle. I admire her gift for giving the lyrical dimension the slip without seeming frivolous. She runs away from tonal pitch as if it were an overbearing suitor.

In Wislawa's poems there is no blood, no setbacks, and no tears resulting from historical vicissitudes. She hits the bull's-eye, as if it were nothing, right in the marrow of issues. She said that she fled from solemn statements because when she wrote she felt she had someone behind her laughing at her. Humility and shyness fuelled her irony.

Yesterday I bumped into a gnome. There are bronze gnomes in some places, the symbol the people chose in the fight against the communist government. I almost broke my nose.

'The joy of writing. The possibility of remaining. The revenge of a mortal hand.' Szymborska's sense of humour.

She's right: we all have a jester behind us making faces, whether we want to see it or not.

San Simon Island, October 2018. Eu non morrerei fremosa no mar maior. It's been so windy these last few days. The wind tore up and dragged away the bark of the eucalyptus trees. The beauty of this place adds to the tragic density of its history. The buildings here were used as lazarettos and as orphanages. I have read that the *Upo Mendi* was anchored here for months, a floating jail packed with republican and Basque nationalist prisoners. During the Franco regime, the island was used as a concentration camp.

San Simon is a symbol of the Galician tradition thanks to a piece by the troubadour Mendinho: *'Non hei barqueiro, nen remador: morrerei eu fremosa no mar maior. Eu atendendo o meu amigo. E verrá?'*

I have no boatman, no rower: I will die trembling on the high seas. I'm looking out for my friend. Will he come?

Pay attention, dear friend: if you don't want to drown in the high seas, you'd better not get tangled with any guys.

The tops of the yew trees have come so close to each other that they form a green arch. On the path stripped of grass, a squirrel watches me.

To live is to go on. I agree.

Lviv, August 2016. Timeless moss. The theatre at the top of the avenue is very similar to the Arriaga Theatre in Bilbao. They built it by burying the river. When the current, like a treacherous snake, began to eat up the foundations – as would anyone persevering until the final victory – the architect committed suicide. On the cornice there is a sculpture of a pregnant woman, an allegory of freedom. Makes sense.

At the flea market they sold toilet paper with Putin's face on it. I bought a hair clip, made with dried flowers, and E.M. several rustic rag dolls. We met yesterday at a reading and I think we feel comfortable together. He's a compelling man, in many respects. The city has gifted me his company.

We talk about Krystyna Rodowska over a beer. *One of the abuses of history is to condemn some things to become mere memory...* I say. E. M. agrees: *Of history with a capital H and of stories in lowercase*. We laugh and search our mobile phones for some verses from the poet: 'The mythical lions no longer care for the memory of so many peoples and languages. / The house from which I was expelled still stands, as I have been told, and is still faithfully visited by its dead.' Exiles.

Poetry doesn't change the world, but sometimes it builds houses. Collective houses and private houses. We know something about that.

What must it be like, to condemn oneself to internal exile?

We went up to the castle, of which there are no ruins left. What is there are television antennas, the antithesis of the idealised playground that Stanislaw Lem describes in *Highcastle*.

Afterwards we visited the Armenian synagogue. And after that the best place against the sweltering heat: the cemetery. It is on a hill, strewn with weeds and brambles like a gothic garden. Moss on the pergolas, on the monoliths, on the statues.

A funeral sculpture catches my eye. I feel towards that image – a veiled woman who, bent over by sadness, collapses on a tomb with a garland of roses in her hands – a feeling of sisterhood. And a remote memory that I can't quite identify makes me feel sorry for myself. It is the most sublime expression of mourning I have ever seen, the representation of desolation, timeless and perennial.

Amsterdam, April 2017. Nomadic bones. A music ensemble plays in Oudekerksplein. My son stops to listen to them. I am happy: there can't be many mothers who spend their holidays in the noble company of their twenty-one-year-old sons. Although it sometimes feels as if my strength is going to fail and I'm going to fall over.

We invited Nadine over to our house to look after Colette. She brought Binoche, of course. When we return I'll have to remove half a ton of cat hair from the sofa.

Organs, stained glass windows, chapels and baptismal fonts under boat-shaped vaults. And slabs etched with figures and letters.

Near the choir, with number 31, Hester Hooft, the girl that Casanova mentions in his memoirs: 'Why my hand?' she asked the pervert. She was eleven years old, less than half his age when he attempted to kiss her.

According to the information panel, in the 18th century they exhumed the remains and piled them up in an ossuary only to re-bury them a few metres further on. The displacement of skeletons is incomprehensible unless you know the reason why: those transfers must have been lucrative, like furniture removals.

I remember that when I was a child, they emptied out the portico of the church in Lekeitio too. Aitita got a skull for my brother, who was studying medicine. Future doctors and seminarians used to keep skulls in their rooms. Whether they led them to deeper meditations or not, I can't tell. The skull Hamlet held in his hand was that of his friend, the jester Yorick; ours was anonymous. My brother pointed out the geography of that skull with its technical names: parietal, occipital, palatal, temporal, frontal. At one point it occurred to me that this piece might belong to the ghost of a woman who wandered the other world headless, and I was overwhelmed by a despicable feeling – that of being an accessory to a desecration.

Miramar, November, 2018. Double visit. I have hiked the Marierrota bidegorri, the path along the tidal mill between the beaches of Isuntza and Karraspio. There was a heron in the marsh, in front of the Zubieta palace. It unknowingly gave me a message: *Lux, Pax, Vis*.

Then I came to the garden house, not without visiting my people in the cemetery first, as is customary today. The bellflowers are trying hard to overwhelm the ground. If we don't put a stop to it, they will suffocate everything else, as pernicious ideas do when they trample the territory of common sense.

I'm meeting T. for the movies. How many movies have we seen together since we were little girls. *The most interesting one, the movie of our lives,* she would tell me, squeezing my hand.

Sincere friendship fills the void of what we don't have. Just as in childhood, when in the calligraphy homework letters gained prominence as we went over the discontinuous lines with our pencils, in this moment I perceive the shape of loneliness: it is exact and clear, the placenta of freedom.

The avocado pit that someone threw from one of the flats across the street is already a little tree. The oleander is lush, but the vine is out of control and the fruit trees, dishevelled, are crying out for pruning. The earth's crust is still tender. Colette rests right there. My holy garden, my holy dead.

Txori Txuri

When your mother's shop moved to the town centre, the premises became a garage and a workshop for the family. The shop windows that Aitita had built in the forties were replaced by a folding garage door for our blue Seat 127. The shelves that used to hold a multitude of rolls of fabric were now home to screw boxes, diesel drums, rolls of rope and wire spools, plugs and tubes, loose handles, fishing lines and hooks, reels of raffia yarn and mechanic and carpentry tools: saws, pliers, gimlets, adjustable wrenches, hammers.

At home the reigning law was not to throw anything away, and a deeply rooted habit not to spend without fore-thought. For people who had known the hardship of war, anything could have a second life. That attachment to the objects of the past as well as the tendency to repurpose old things is within you too. That is why, for example, you apply yourself to the task of restoring the headboard, bedside tables and other pieces in your old bedroom, trying to give a modern look to all that furniture that fashion left behind.

The shop that you have just emptied to put on the market retains a certain glow in your memory,, like a forest in autumn. It must be because of the farmers who used to come and buy apparel: aprons, underwear, socks, mantillas, sailors' blue canvas cloth by the metre. They readily accepted your mother's recommendations and trusted her advice. The shop had history; it had been opened by a great-aunt and your godmother, seamstresses who'd left their farm-house before the war to settle in the village.

That's why your mother always had a warm welcome for the farmers of Mendexa, Oleta, Amoroto, Gizaburuaga, Ispaster.

She helped them introduce modernity into their traditional trousseau: leatherette, acrylic, nylon, suede. Conversely, French tourists came looking for old-fashioned tablecloths and embroidered sheets, nostalgic for handcrafted products. You acted as an interpreter even though you were a child and only half understood what they were saying.

It has taken you many hours to go through everything that had accumulated in the shop for decades. That habit of keeping everything is a torment. Why, given that nobody can take anything over to the other side and it's always up to those left behind to clean it all up in the end. You have organised three piles: the first, useless rubbish; the second, recyclable items; and the third – a more voluminous pile than you would have hoped; but you are sentimental, aren't you, and those souvenirs stick to your hands – objects that mean something to you.

A suitcase appears from beneath some moth-eaten coats. Its contents take you to a long-lost place; to a point hidden under many layers and events; to an ellipsis. It is a bundle of Sam notebooks, millimetre series, with realistic illustrations of animals on their orange covers: carp, rattlesnake, koala, dragonfly, bird of paradise.

Your mother kept them – just as your grandfather kept fragments of saints – thinking that they might have some use one day. Most are dated between September 1973 and 1978. You wrote *Mon Premier Cahier de Français* on the cover of one of them. You like to imagine that, although there are thirteen volumes, you meant to conceive the collection as a unit, as tends to be the way with life's lessons: lots of scraps, a single canvas.

You were good at memorising vocabulary lists, numbered words with their corresponding and classified meanings: *noms, adjectifs, verbs, adverbs, locutions*. Corrections, to be repeated ten times. You never imagined that you would one day profit from that traditional language-learning system of repetition and end up translating children's books. Your family, who invested their faith in your education, would sigh to the heavens if they could see that their girl has no fixed salary, like so many artists, nor does she have a union that can get her out of a tough spot. That's the price of taking risks, don't be surprised. Every morning you repeat your pentalogue like a mantra before getting up: trust your choice, do it your way, keep showing up, be brave, onward.

Onward, your godfather's motto. He used to bring you brochures for student exchanges from the travel agents: Grenoble, Reims, Arles, Lille, Toulouse. He was willing to gift you a course abroad, like he gifted you a trinket upon returning from each trip, little medallions with your zodiac sign, your wedding dress, Miramar, or that last look the morning he died in your arms.

But the women of the house were wary of sending their girl abroad, lest she lose her way and return with an unwanted package. And besides, you had to help in the shop in July and August. Things being what they were, playing pretend-to-be-French became your favourite game. In the summer you renamed yourself, reborn as an actress: Lissette, Jacqueline, Marie Jeanne, Régine, Noelle. Your heart was a French notebook at seventeen, a hotbed of unsuspected longings.

One afternoon in early June you went down to study at the pier. You still like to think outdoors with your books and papers. You sat on the stone steps with your notes.

A sailboat came in, *Txori txuri*, white bird. She carried the French flag and the Basque ikurrina, which at the end of the seventies was everywhere on backpacks, key rings, umbrellas, purses, T-shirts. There was also a proliferation of garments printed with Basque symbols: the lauburu, the ancient tree of Gernika, the *ezpata-dantza* or sword dance, the map of Euskal Herria, slogans such as *Nik euskaraz* – meaning: I (do everything) in Basque.

The ship docked near where you were. You heard her occupants speak and asked them if they'd mind letting you see inside. They invited you to dinner. It never crossed your mind to think that they might kidnap you, rape you and throw you overboard into the sea like the girl in the ballad you had recently analysed in Basque class. You made the correct choice when you mentioned that you had read *Le Comte de Monte-Cristo* during the school year; an adapted version, of course. This detail added points to your charm, because their dog was named Dumas.

At half past ten at night you ran home and endured the downpour of reproaches without complaint: *How could you just trust some strangers! Where's your brain! We were so worried! You should have warned us! Thank God you're back in one piece!*

There was no reason to worry, they were good people. The next day they showed up at the shop. Do you remember their names? Let's say the parents were Chantal and Luc, both health professionals in a hospital; the son, Patrick, a boy your age; and Marie, an eight-year-old girl. She has often visited you in dreams under different guises: white dove, dwarf heron, snow goose, holy spirit, secret swan.

Marie spoke into her mother's ear. She had long, light brown hair, and carried with her a certain sense of orphanhood. You still didn't know that she barely slept, that she suffered phobias, that she had a complex that held her back, that her nerves tormented her, that her imagination was a treacherous compass. The day before, while dining on the boat, she had rested her cheek on your arm.

Mother and daughter bought bikinis. Father and son wanted swimming trunks, but you didn't have them. To justify the lack, you explained to them that the men here didn't fancy that style, that they wore sports shorts to the beach.

They planned to stay a week and asked if you might be free to accompany them to Gernika. You accepted on condition of returning before closing time, as it was your job to tidy and sweep up the shop. My godfather gave you a booklet titled *Temas Vascos* that described the ornamental richness of the Casa de Juntas. You would act as a tour guide. You weren't going to visit France that year either, but a family wearing sailor jumpers had arrived from the pier in Cap Breton ready to practise French with you.

On the outskirts of the town there was a cliff that was reached through a slope bordered by sea fennel and *Armeria euscadiensis*, a native carnation that grew along the coast. An immense slab of rock stretched out alongside a cove filled with boulders like toasted almonds, quail eggs, fresh beans, buttermilk rolls, condensed milk droplets. You wanted to show Patrick this place, and the falcon family that nested on its slopes. Jean was reluctant to let you go alone; Chantal, on the other hand, encouraged Marie. It'd be healthy for her not to be stuck to her parents for a while.

While crossing the fern grove, the child slipped, and a wet mark was imprinted on her pink bikini. You took her by the hand and kept walking down. Particles of dirt got into your sandals.

In a tidal pool you found crabs, anemones, a sea urchin, snails, a starfish. It was missing a leg and you thought it somehow resembled the child. You filled a basket with limpets to cook later in parsley sauce.

'What happened to your eye? It looks like you've been

punched, or like bleach went into your eye,' Patrick asked as you lay down on a rock.

You explained that you had lost it five years earlier, that you almost went blind, that you had surgery last April, that you hadn't been able to join your class' study trip, that it didn't hurt anymore.

Dumas watched uneasily as a group of cormorants flew in and out of the gulf.

You didn't see her, neither of you saw her. It was your first time feeling someone else's saliva in your mouth, a hand in your hair, a commotion, a sting, an influx of desire. Then yes, barking. You got up suddenly. You ran to the break.

Among the waves danced two pink blots and a skein of hair that looked like amber seaweed, runaway bridles, elastic yarns, stray rays, the threads of destiny. The swell swayed the body that floated upside down like a clumsy white bird that had spread its wings, mistaking the sea for the sky.

You screamed. You waved your arms hoping to attract the attention of the boats catching squid right ahead of you, in the segment of the horizon that in that twilight hour looked like a blade.

One of your godfather's colleagues drove you to the funeral in his van. You crossed Irun, Hendaia, Doinbane Lohizune, Bidart, Baiona.

The coffin, loaded with lilies on a catafalque, looked like a rowing boat decked out for a maritime feast. When you approached to offer your condolences, you thought Patrick's swollen eyelids looked like larvae, slugs, glands, lobes, molluscs. He turned his back on you. You staggered. Chantal raised her hand, don't get any closer.

Aitabitxi put the radio on in the journey back. He sat in the front; Ama and you in the back. You'd spent the last few days babbling absurd phrases like *Je vous salue, Marie* or singing without pause *Se equivocó la paloma, se equivocaba.* The dove got it wrong, got it wrong... Your nails were bleeding. Your mother put her arm around your shoulders, but the weight of her dismay was so overwhelming that a shiver ran through you both.

You made a stop en route. My godfather wanted to buy a few things for his supper club, the *txoko: bloc de foie gras, brique de chèvre, crème fraiche, vin de Bordeaux, escargots à la Bourguignonne.* Those sporadic epicurean outbursts were a sign of his determination to keep savouring our good luck no matter what. He came back carrying plastic bags full of food through the downpour. Onward.

'Caprice des dieux,' he said, reaching out for you to pick up a container of cheese with two little angels on its lid. Camembert.

You burst into tears for the first time since the event.

But the hardest part was over. And the closer you got to the frontier, the more the cream's texture, the burst of its flavour, its invigorating aroma, the smoothness of its crust, the aptness of its name comforted you.

You understood that from then on it would depend on you – and on the whim of the gods – what you learnt from the things that happened in your life. And that it was going to be a challenge, that you'd fight with yourself, you'd periodically review your passions, your commitments, and there'd be tears. Maybe you would be a French teacher in some years' time; maybe you'd be a translator, although this was unthinkable for now; or, maybe, who's to know, you'd be a writer, to tell all this.

La Vita è Bella

1. Between Leaks

If you want to write, have a cat.
– Aldous Huxley

Colette came home at the end of the year. Only until spring. That was the deal.

In fact, my son had brought him over a couple of months earlier, when he was the size of a fist. His fur was tan and white, and he had a dark mole on his muzzle. That was what I loved the most, the asymmetry of his face. And his slight squint.

I've never felt drawn to animals: they either scared me or disgusted me. But on that day the tenderness with which my boy soothed the animal moved me, because he reminded me of my mother when she held her newborn grandson in her arms.

'Okay, it's fine for today,' I relented, 'but you're taking him back tomorrow.'

I sensed that sooner or later I'd be looking after him. I'm always going back and forth with my suitcase, my computer and work materials, and I wasn't willing to add the cat basket to that as well.

'We can leave him in Miramar, Amatxu. And that'll be the end of the rats.'

But the cold December weather made me feel sorry for the kitten, because the poor thing spent hours locked in the little house in the orchard, and so I let him stay with us while the weather improved.

'We'll call him Colette.'

'But he's male!'

'That doesn't matter. Maybe he'll bring me inspiration with that name.'

I put together some toys and got him a bowl for his water, and even turned on the Christmas lights in the bay window as a welcome ceremony. As soon as I opened the door, the cat headed into the living room, where my desk leans against a bookcase built by my grandfather. There's a box under the table where I keep a couple of shawls I wear when it gets chilly. Colette curled up in that exact spot.

That's how he won me over, because of the place he chose (I didn't know then that kitties love all boxes). I thought him intelligent, that's the thing, because the box, which a Polish friend had hand-painted for me, has this line written on it: *La vita è bella*.

Beautiful, indeed, is life.

When I looked in the mirror in the morning, I saw that my left eye had turned around. Proof if any was needed of the anguish I'd experienced during the night.

I'd had a nightmare.

On the island of Lekeitio. A stormy night, just like in a scary movie. O. and I face to face shouting at each other, but the crash of the waves drowns out our voices. A gust of wind knocks us and we fall face down: me on the grass; him, on the edge of the precipice. I put my arms out to hold him. *Grab me, hold on,* I tell him. In vain. He disappears into the void. I panic. I don't want to see his body wrecked against the reef. My wrists are dislocated, they hurt a lot. I finally dare to look down. I see that his fall was not fatal: O. is sitting astride a rock, surrounded by foam. Little by little, the rock begins to move as if it were a canoe and carries him away while he helps things along by paddling with his arms. He doesn't look up, he doesn't even raise his hand to wave goodbye.

I couldn't tell him my nightmare because he'd left me. 'I want to be alone.'

We had settled into the folds of mediocrity, sick of not trying to make each other happy. Despite this, the suddenness of his decision threw me.

Parting ways is always difficult, at least for me it is. I am not going to go into details: it'd be pathetic to get into the variants of pain again.

Pain cannot be allowed to take control.

I decided to move to my flat in Bilbao for a few months.

I would take refuge in work and strengthen ties with the city. I wasn't feeling well at all, but if I'd been able to take part in the Korrika benefit race's celebratory *lip dub* the day after the breakup... Shoulder your sorrows and take a step forward. 'What matters is not the intensity with which we've been crushed; what matters is the intensity we are left with after being crushed.' That's what Gonçalo M. Tavares says in his *Voyage to India*.

I'm used to being there, in the gallery of heartbreak. Its walls are too slippery to climb, it's impossible to get over to the other side. If it were possible we would hit that invisible construction until it fell, but that's not something that can be done with hammers: it's the mind that must be changed through continuous effort in order to jump through the traps in the labyrinth. Happiness – the memory of happiness we carry – is sticky and clings to the skin. And to everything else.

I knew that I would have to take the pain and resentment with both hands, and that I would have to knead them, make a ball and swallow it until it became one with my metabolism and I expelled it little by little. I knew that I would be the one to pick up the bones of our history, the one to burn them.

I noticed the whitish stain as soon as I opened the door. It looked like sugar... Or powdered milk. But as soon as I put the suitcases down I realised that the stain was the result of a leak.

The paintings were full of cloudy trails, as if lizards had paraded around them. The floor was bulging and some planks had even fractured. In the waterlogged kitchen I stepped on something that looked like liquid caramel. Scraps of wallpaper hung like limp banners here and there. Plaster dust coated the induction cooker. The clock had stopped.

Nice irony: just when you urgently need to tend to your psychic habitat, your physical space is in tatters.

'Water came through again,' I told the neighbour.

The incident was more serious than the previous one, when faeces leaked into my bathroom.

After a dance of mops and washcloths I sat in the armchair to contemplate the disaster.

I was sad about all the water. Sad about the breakup. Sad also because I hadn't managed to bring Colette to me: he'd clawed at me as I tried to put him in the carrier and I'd had to give up, clumsy me. The whole thing made me feel helpless.

The following morning I sat in front of my computer determined to continue with my project, postponed time and time again. It didn't have a title yet, but I intuited that the idea of bones could make sense in the context of my work (because it traces a path that begins on the skin, continues on the hands and momentarily contemplates the eye in the context of an inquiry that aims to reach the innermost strata).

My son showed up a couple of days later with Colette, who went straight to the study and jumped on my chair, where he curled into a ball – I don't know whether he did so attracted by the aura of my computer, or by my perfume.

It's difficult to understand the bonds we forge with pets until they're tested by our own lived experience.

We went out for dinner in the neighbourhood Chinese. Despite the setbacks and upsets, life was beautiful, of course. The visit was cheering. Still, when I looked at the three women sitting at the next table, eating in complete silence, I was reminded of that haunting question in Chekhov's *Three Sisters*: 'Life is beautiful, yes. But what if it just seems like it is?'

Repairs began. If it wasn't the builder, it was the painter; if it wasn't the painter, it was the carpenter who was at home; or the plumber, or the surveyor. Overwhelmed and without peace of mind, I struggled to move forward with my things, as if I were walking barefoot on arid land. Life, sometimes, is a cunning shoe thief.

Colette would miaow at six in the morning. He jumped from the bed to the dresser, from the dresser to the wardrobe and from the wardrobe to the bed. His wailing made my hair stand on end, and it made me cringe to see him continuously licking his parts. His frenzied spurts of pee made my couch indecent.

I called the clinic and took him there at the appointed time, feeling very much like how I used to feel when I took my child to the paediatrician. I cursed at the vet when he stuck the syringe in him without even trying to calm him down a little beforehand.

'I'll call you around five. Once the anaesthetic wears off, he'll be as good as new. We'll fix him in a jiffy.'

But the cat was a soggy husk when I went to pick him up. I was close to snapping at the man and asking if he only knew how to care for cattle, but I bit my tongue and went home feeling like a *mater dolorosa*.

I opened the carrier. Colette stumbled and fell on his

side several times, leaving a trickle of blood on the kitchen tiles, so I wrapped him up in his nap blanket. He didn't move. Maybe he was too young for the operation?

I saw myself reflected in him: his helplessness, the feeling of overall pain difficult to pinpoint, the need for an arm on the shoulder: self-pity is an almost inevitable reaction, unless the distortions of thought are analysed.

The rain seemed grey against the windows.

'We both have to get over this, *txiki*.'

I lit a scented candle and the smell of mint purified the room. I would have gladly smoked a menthol cigarette as a consolation prize.

In *Alias Grace*, Margaret Atwood writes: 'When you are in the middle of a story it isn't a story at all, but only a confusion; a dark roaring, a blindness, a wreckage of shattered glass and splintered wood; like a house in a whirlwind, or else a boat crushed by the icebergs or swept over the rapids, and all aboard powerless to stop it. It's only afterwards that it becomes anything like a story at all. When you are telling it, to yourself or to someone else.'

I think that's what I am doing.

Miramar had turned into a jungle. We hadn't tended to it since the spring.

'My friends said they'll help clear the scrub,' my son announced.

'Oh great... if you take care of the land, I'll take care of the little house.'

Between Adela and I, we dust and clear the cobwebs. Although small, the plot and little house are a lot of work and, since I don't like asking favours, it's increasingly problematic for me to manage it: I'm satisfied with keeping the weeds at bay.

The palm tree at least was healthy.

I sent a message to a few friends to invite them for a light meal under the palm-frond awning on the eve of San Juan.

Life sometimes claps at us: everyone sent their apologies. I'm not the centre of the world I guess.

The thing is that I, who, like anyone else, have lost a bit of everything, used to boast about never having lost any friends. But that afternoon I began to question the meaning of friendship.

We want to believe that we would never put up with certain things, that we would not accept them under any pretext, and yet we constantly do so. We find excuses to forgive the mistakes others make with us as a strategy not to reveal our own shortcomings.

When I got back home Colette wasn't there. He used to appear in the hallway, ready to escape. I worried when I realised I had left the back balcony open: it wouldn't be the first time he'd run away. I was conscious of my tone as I called him, it was embarrassing; I sounded desperate, to tell the truth. His name echoed in the lane.

A mass of negative thoughts began to scratch my conscience. *This is my fault. I haven't cared for him properly. I couldn't bear to lose him. He's going to run away with the street cats.* A litany of abandonment, applicable both to cats and two-legged beings.

Colette came out from behind a chest of drawers only after I'd grown hoarse from all the whining and cooing. I whispered sweet things to him that I won't repeat here to maintain my dignity. It was then that we signed our pact of fidelity.

I locked myself in. O Bosom of Silence! Oh, Erotica of Creation! This version of me, anchored to my pages, was an acceptable companion for the cat; the cat, with his purrs and his rubs, a perfect presence for this me.

Colette was not as pragmatic as the mouser described by William S. Burroughs: 'I am the cat who walks alone. / And to me all supermarkets are alike. / The cat does not offer services. / The cat offers itself.'

I was no ordinary supermarket either.

2. Ignis Fatuus

You're wondering if I'm lonely [...]
If I'm lonely
it's with the rowboat ice-fast on the shore
in the last red light of the year
that knows what it is, that knows it's neither
ice nor mud nor winter light
but wood, with a gift for burning
– Adrienne Rich (from 'Song')

Rats hide away to die once they have tasted poison. That wasn't my predicament, but I was suffering like someone who's been poisoned. I got sick.

Despite heading my reasoning in the right direction, my body rebelled against me. A dull discomfort in my stomach, or in my intestines, or in my uterus wouldn't leave me alone – I didn't know which organ it was that was whipping me, but I burned with pain. My body manifested the symptoms of the transition between situation A (a failed relationship), and situation B (the anguish of trying to bridge the gap between theory and practice, my reluctance to accept set-backs, a certain listlessness in the soul, and so on).

'I can't anymore,' I complained to J. 'Take me to hospital, or to a mental asylum, I don't care.'

'Forget about either. We're going to the valley of Baztan for the weekend.'

Shortly after arriving at the inn we met two of her friends – she'd called them in advance – who made me lie down on the bed. The older one rubbed my forehead with a handkerchief; the other rubbed the scars on my belly, wounds from old surgeries.

'I can feel the knots,' she said.

She explained something about the hands of the clock

and asked if I knew a plant called San Inazio's bean, that it'd be good for me to take it. I said I didn't: I'm an expert on saints but know nothing about botany.

'Tomorrow we'll bring you some of our own apples. You'll feel it in the stomach above all, apple juice protects the viscera.'

I took my first nap in a long time, aided by the murmur of the trees coming through the window, near the ruins of Donamaria's tower house.

And so, one misfortune gave way to another. What would become of us if they didn't alternate?

The ocularist didn't tell me anything that I didn't already know: an operation was necessary; otherwise, my left eye socket would be irredeemably closed.

Although I had always kind of thought that at some point an eye patch would add a certain exoticism to my look, something like Madame Staël's turban, the certainty of the irreversible hurt. My question surprised the doctor:

'Would you recommend that to me if I were your mother, your wife, or your daughter?'

'If you were, your eye would be fixed already.'

'All right. In any case, I'd like to finish the book I'm working on before the surgery.'

How, though?

Back in my student days I used to fill pages without fore-thought: the simple act of starting to write made ideas flow; now, however, I was at a standstill.

I was like Colette, playing with invisible things. Sometimes he would crouch in front of the bedside table and lie in wait, as if there were something hidden underneath; other times he jumped as if, having spotted a shape inside the light, he wanted to chase it.

My diary began to fill up with random fragments.

Virginia Woolf: 'You cannot find peace by avoiding life.'

Your homeopath would tell you: 'Release ballast weight.' Your ophthalmologist would tell you: 'Focus on the operation'. Any employee of the Lanbide jobcentre would tell you: 'Aren't you ashamed to complain seeing the shit people have to live with?'. The Director of Cruces Hospital would tell you: 'Go ahead and take a stroll on any floor.' Your neighbour would ask: 'Don't you watch TV?'

From Urbion, B. has sent me a photo of an eguzki-lore, the protective Basque thistle flower: 'It sends you good light.' Should I believe in such things?

Bukowski extolled the ability of cats to spend twenty hours sleeping: 'These creatures are my teachers.' Colette, master of the *dolce vita*... I wouldn't get very far if I were to live your life of leisure.

He's being weird though. Did he get depressed because of the rain? Or is he unwell too?

My son calls me from Bilbao:

'Don't get upset...'

'What happened? Are you okay?'

'Yes, I am, but we have another flood. Come as soon as possible.'

The house has turned into a river. God help me.

The previous time I took advantage of the repairs to paint my room white. It seemed a good way to erase the emotional scars left by the men with whom I had shared my intimacy. The water has drawn mould flowers on the bedspread. I laughed when I saw my Emily Dickinson-esque décor turned into a caricature.

G., listening to my repertoire of troubles, displays the optimism that characterises her:

'You'll break this cycle.'

'I feel like my feet are in a quagmire. Always the same wounds, the same problems, again and again.'

'Even if you don't feel it, time is never still. Even the hermit in the tarot advances, with his cane and the lamp in his hand... Like you. You can't see his feet under his tunic and he seems motionless but still, he walks.'

'I see. And at this rate, I'll get a grey beard like his, too.'

I've put new batteries in all the dead clocks at home.

The metamorphosis is about to begin. Objective: kill the hamster. You have been turning and turning blindly inside the wheel for too long, stuck inside the inertia of a Ferris wheel. Everything is (and has been) an absurd repetition.

Some species of insects, amphibians, molluscs, crustaceans, cnidarians and echinoderms undergo trans-formations. But you don't visualise jellyfish, frogs or butterflies in the time you spend collapsed on the sofa. You see a snake that bites its own tail forming a circle: the ouroboros, a circle circling within a circle; a symbol of senseless struggle, the cyclical nature of events and the impossibility of something new beginning despite all efforts.

A butterfly in the elevator. Good omen. No, it's a moth. That makes more sense. It felt like she was making fun of me: 'I'm a moth, a damsel of the night. I flee from the flame, full of fortune.'

Does someone with only a small fire inside ever feel cold? Not necessarily.

Amanda drags me to Bilbao's Karola Crane. It doesn't matter if it's drizzling or if there's a downpour. She really is a crane for me. Although her real name is another, I call her Amanda because of her ability to ease everything. Guide to the blind, always propping things up.

Circles are hypnotic. To escape hypnosis, I focus on linear images: motorway lanes, the horizon, spools of thread, streamers, things like that.

I also make lists. They help me break the circle. For example, a list of depressive turns that must be avoided: do not keep fabric softener in the fridge; do not lose keys twenty times a day; do not wait ten minutes for the lift without having pressed the button; do not see an O. clone three times in the same place...

Jenny Holzer: 'Old friends are better left in the past.'

What does it mean to be a friend? Being there. And continuing to be there.

I swim. One hundred strokes, one hundred and fifty, two hundred strokes, two hundred and fifty... In each stroke, my spell: 'Independence, independence...'. My mantra sounds like a political demand. Sometimes I see people I'd rather not see. I repeat another incantation every time I feel that pinch in my chest: 'Look towards the light!'

People with burns stay away from cold water too.

I walk in the sand drawing lines as straight as possible with my footprints (to break the circle). A wide-brimmed hat and dark glasses are my allies so that no one dares approach to interrupt my interior monologue.

I run into some acquaintances. Condolences on the recent death of their father.

'How is your mum doing?'

'We've taken her to a home ... she has dementia now and won't stop moving, spinning around.... We were going crazy.'

Round and round, back and forth, just like a mechanical toy. Poor thing, I thought. Flora, too, walked in circles the last few times I visited her in the hospice.

I have spent the most important day of the festival, Antzar Eguna – Day of the Geese – in the fields of Urbia, at a thousand metres of altitude (the fog was thick, I didn't see God). I'm alone. A-lone. Alone-alone-alone.

Within the island of voluntary isolation there is another islet, that of your own insatiable loneliness. Often, you act as if you didn't know it. Not owning that is cheating.

L. came.

'Shall we go to the concert?'

I accept any invitation, but wherever I go, I come back heavy with a weight that feels like false gold.

'I don't know...'

'Why ever not! Why don't you try to see yourself from a different perspective? Changing perspective leads us to changing ourselves.'

She put her finger on it.

'Easy to say... You don't seem to care about my suffering.'

'You have to scrape the wound to clean it. And then sew it well so that it closes,' she answers, gesturing like a diligent seamstress.

It's obvious that she is a doctor.

I don't have enough handkerchiefs. A crybaby feminist, the finest artist.

When will all this become a film without images. When will the new days dawn, free of old chains.

'All sorrows can be borne if you put them into a story,' Karen Blixen wrote in her letters from Africa.

But I'm wearing down my nails from undoing so many of my knots.

Writing is also about moving in a circle: I turn around my own axis and I turn around my story. Rotation and translation, the movement of consternation.

Can interpreting nightmares be therapeutic? I do it with the caution of the peasants of the Middle Ages who nailed doors and windows to prevent the plague from invading the village.

Umpteenth dream...

In an operating room. O. and I lie face down on two stretchers, covered with a sheet. It's terribly cold. As the surgeon approaches, O. raises his arm and says, 'Me first.'

First goes first.

Where does the seed of balance germinate? In the wasteland fertilised by difficulties (that plague, O.'s abandonment, the thousand leaks, my sick body)? Or in the little plot of land delimited by the milestones of my choosing (my son, my writing, my cat, my friends)?

'Sometimes it's important to be radical.'

'True, if the goal is your own well-being,' E. replies.

This is how we ate the two trays of sushi that she brought: radically.

Ignis fatuus, or will-o'-the-wisp. Although it might seem magic, it is a simple chemical phenomenon. Back in the day, those bluish or yellow flames that people saw in the dark were the souls that, not being allowed to enter purgatory, still roamed the world.

Cemeteries were the ideal places to find them because the phosphorus in the bones, when it meets the air, releases a gas that glows at a short distance from the ground. Swamps and lagoons are good places too, as they are rich in decomposing organic matter.

Does this explanation manage to convey that we too are will-o'-the-wisps? We learn to get out of bad situations; to internalise the absence of those we lose; to disbelieve that love is everything; to play at deciphering signs; to give ourselves one more chance for anything; to accept the losses and gains that come with the passage of time.

On our chests, like inscriptions on a medal, we carry our guiding paths. Until suddenly life comes and blows out the flame and its light.

You've chosen the most suitable remnant you saved when your mother closed the shop: a brown, white and grey plaid fleece that matches Colette's fur.

Last night you woke up breathing heavily and with a dry mouth, unsettled by the worries that you took to bed. 02:20. You put on your robe and went to the hallway without turning on the light. You heard your son's soft snores in the corridor.

Colette was awake too. His eyes half-closed and his pupils dilated. You know that look: you first saw it as a child on a dying dolphin on the beach.

You tried giving him the antibiotic mixed with yoghurt, but he wouldn't swallow it. He licked your hand. However, when you caressed him, he hissed at you. He crawled to a fresh towel that you placed on the rug. A pained miaow. You spoke a few words to him, the kind we say when nobody hears us.

Back in bed, a familiar singsong enveloped you: the creaking of wood, unintelligible voices, moans, a vague commotion inside your own head: the warp of noises you heard as you said goodbye to your elders, that misshapen murmur that can only be heard during stern vigils, as if a phantom merry-go-round were going round and round in the dark.

To laugh or cry? I love you, Nina Simone.

Another list: *Ain't got no air. Ain't got no faith. Ain't got no man. Ain't got no love. Ain't got no mother. Ain't got no father. Ain't got no brother. Ain't got no aunts. Ain't got no uncles. Ain't got no friends. Ain't got no veil...*

I've got my eye. I've got my skin. I've got myself. I've got life. I've got my lives.

A spark in his eyes. The end.

I have taken him to Miramar wrapped in the tricoloured cloth. I picked periwinkles by the front wall, the earliest winter flowers. But we dug his grave in the sunniest part, in the spot that cats that come from other orchards like. The toy seagull went into the grave too, but without its sound box. My son places some old tiles that we had been keeping in the shed on top of Colette.

'In case a fox visits. So it won't be tempted to stir up the earth... it might eat his remains.'

Colette. 2017-2018. *Requiescat in pace.*

When I return home, I clean up the *La vita è bella* box and put it back under my desk, full of blank pages.

Ain't got no cat.

3. Regarding Distance

Nothing but a cold, beautiful waste.
– Andrzej Stasiuk (from *On the Road to Babadog: Travels in the Other Europe*)

We can brag about this or that, but it is much easier to fix a thousand problems of any kind than a shattered heart. But this is something we only acknowledge in hushed tones.

I don't know if that proverb is of my own making or if it stuck to me somewhere.

While crossing the barren gorge of pain, and sometimes even after, leaving becomes the truest goal of someone who's been trapped. Responding to the instinct to leave with action sustains dignity – or something like it, in any case.

According to Rachel Cusk's character in *Kudos*, 'all I knew was that [suffering] carried a kind of honour, if you survived it, and left you in a relationship to the truth that seemed closer, but that in fact might have been identical to the truthfulness of staying in one place.'

The title of the novel is *Prestigio* in Spanish; weaker than the original, in my opinion, since the Greek *kudos* means fame or glory (Homer, for example, uses it to describe the magic powers of heroes). It is a gorgeous paradox that we ordinary creatures – antiheroes – believe we've triumphed just by sticking to our principles when faced by conflict.

Distance is my place

Distance is my place.

Right here I can lay my spoils
on columns of air
and spit on false gods.
Their voices scratch me from behind
when I set out to plant flowers
or watch the cormorant contemplate the wind.

Here freedom equals
intestinal pain,
Saturday night from a window,
creaking bones without a pet,
slow breaths with a taste of *Lachesis Mutus*,
a black and white butterfly crushed on the asphalt.

Saltpetre diffuses my shadow on the sidewalks
(this means that my friends don't mention me
and eventually we all believe I never existed).

Out there, the waltz of the spheres sounds like a merry-go-round,
but who is that melody for?
For those who never cross hell alone
or arrange their return before taking off.

I host conferences with myself
in empty rooms where words demand a reward:
wanted, wanted, wanted.
With my heart in a trap and stars in my brain,
I bite through filaments and chains
while I decide what to do with the memory of happiness.

Distance is my place now.

I have managed to hold back the dastardliest fear of them all, the fear of becoming isolated. I see warnings in some glances. *Do you know what happens to kites when their string breaks? They lurch onward on their own, but crash sooner or later.*

Do I have the gift of metacognition? I attribute to others the gossip I make up about myself.

I tell myself that I wish a hurricane would take me and drag me far away.

No, I am not a kite: I am a meteorite.

I was a satellite before, but my cosmos has become obsolete.

We stopped many times along the mountain, especially from the vantage point onwards. M. J. takes photos of everything: the grass, the stones, the cliff side that can be glimpsed through the holm oak forest. It's my first time at the summit of Mount Otoio. An orange butterfly flutters around the cement pylon that marks the highest point.

'Is this all?'

'What did you expect?'

I don't know whether this feeling of disenchantment will remain when I leave this obstacle course behind... In my fantasies I see myself garlanded with laurels, wearing the sash of triumph.

M.J. explains to me that, for her, reaching this peak is a way of taking some distance.

'There have been days when I've climbed up here three times. When you are sick of everything...'

'You're incredible.'

'Next time we'll come at dusk. There are different sounds then.'

'You are my best trainer.'

'And you my best entertainer.'

It's true. She had to hold my hand to help me walk through the crags. Also, I vomited three times. My belly aches a lot today.

'That stomach pain is still going on? That's not normal.'

'I'm used to the pain.'

'That isn't normal either.'

The ache is similar to menstrual pain, but focused on the right side.

When we get home I crash into the bed, defeated.

My period disappeared a long time ago. But this body that shows the effects of the laws of gravity still retains its usual passion: loneliness has not soured my blood yet.

I long for a companion sometimes; other times I think it might be more hygienic to be alone. I don't mean this bitterly.

What if I coined an original label for women like me? Expert women, let's say.

I am an expert. We are experts.

It's not a derogatory designation, but ironic, humorous, empathic.

It's ironic because it denotes our experience in key situations. We're used to dealing with things.

It's humorous because it suggests we no longer possess the grace of youth, but that's not really a concern compared to cholesterol, diabetes, osteoarthritis, or high blood pressure.

It is empathetic because it reveals that more than one of us has been used badly, to convenience others, and we have made rookie mistakes.

Stop. The whip of self-flagellation accelerates the speed of the wheel of unproductivity.

I could say 'new women' instead of 'experts'. Or what about 'novices'?

No. It's a hackneyed qualifier and stinks of emotional enthusiasm; the second option is tenderer: it sounds tentative and practical.

After all, we will never get a *cum laude* grade in apprenticeship.

Stop. These ramblings lead nowhere.

Come on, sleep, become my master.

I am in the age of prefixes. I trust that pre-particles will send me in the right direction.

I fall asleep making a mental list: retract, unglue, deactivate, dismantle, unlearn, disconnect, detoxify, disarm, disarm...

I feel better. I would gladly part my thighs to welcome a man in the full midday sun.

In these nebulous intervals of sleeplessness I glimpse images bound to a momentarily unconnected discourse. For example, I am now remembering a little African song that girls sing as they clap their hands, first slapping them on the ground, then on their legs, breasts and face in succession: 'Let there be peace and happiness between my thighs. / May they create and make you go crazy. / May the man whose head rests on my breasts / never wake up'.

May a man fall asleep on my breasts... But not from boredom, *mon Dieu*!

I have a Picasso watercolour on my dresser, *Two Nudes and a Cat*. The man buries his head in the woman's sex while a cat watches. Oh, Colettetxu, how I miss you!

Colette – who despite being a street cat had learned good manners – didn't scratch my bedroom door when I left him in the corridor to host O. I'd be lying if I said that by the end of it my body was an overflowing glass of champagne, but I had more than enough bubbles.

On New Year's Eve I deliberately didn't buy grapes. Love

can be compared to a bunch: it's beautiful as a whole, but pitiful when its elements are dispersed. We lacked an irreplaceable one: faith. I know that's not enough to unite two lovers forever, but it's essential if they're not to abandon one another.

I've only had one cat. Colette, the real one, had a collection of them: Franchette, Pinichette, Kiki-la-Doucette, Mini-mini... And the most special, at least when it comes to its name: One and Only.

One and Only. Unique.

O squared. Like my O.

O. like a circle, a hole, a ring, a wheel, a bullet hole.

O. like the number zero.

A dream in my brief sleep.

In a taxi. I travel with my mother, who caresses my hair as she tells me: 'Don't worry, it's all over... It's over...' I would like to think that this beautiful taxi was life.

It is less complicated to solve any mishap, inconvenience or disaster than to rehabilitate a shattered heart.

4. The Cat's Last Testament

Despite it all, life was beautiful and to be alive too
even when we noted down
the cruel lists of losses,
let's cross together, love,
the last meadow, the last garden.
– Xabier Lete (from 'Song XX')

The plasterer has come to fix the crack in the ceiling of the bay window. My upstairs neighbours had nothing to do with this disaster – I'm glad to report.

'Buildings move; if they didn't, they'd break in half,' he explains. 'The natural intelligence of buildings is exemplary.'

The sentence was haunting me when I ran into an acquaintance on the subway, the father of a former classmate of my son. His face darkened.

'Is everything okay?'

He touched his tie as he answered:

'Well, no. I'm looking for a job. I just got out of an interview. At our age, can you imagine...'

His wife is a housewife, and the girl has not yet finished her studies. The threat of that other kind of crack overwhelmed me: human, static solidity about to collapse. I wished him luck with forced optimism.

I decide to go to A's farmhouse. A surprise. I haven't heard from her in a long time and get the feeling that something is wrong. She also has a tendency to retire to her 'attic' – her gloomy islet – when a setback is too fierce. She doesn't look out the window when she hears my car and takes a while to open the door. She's thinner.

'I don't need permission to come to see you, do I?'

Her eyes moisten.

'You know you don't.'

I see almost-dry buckets of paint in the hallway.

'I started to paint the house, but couldn't do it.'

'And couldn't you call?'

'I have to do it by myself.'

'You can't always do everything by yourself.'

'But it's what I want.'

'What are you like... No wonder you're exhausted. You've been alone for years, you and your strength.'

She offers me her cup without pouring another one for me. I take a sip.

Sitting on the sofa and wrapped in a blanket, A. reads the question on my face.

'I've lost my joy... Time just passes and passes some more.'

We keep silent.

'It's just that sometimes our courage fails us. How about I stay until Sunday? We could get up early and paint. The two of us.'

'Yeah right.'

'Do you remember what I was like when my computer was stolen? You have to bare your teeth at bad luck, seventy times seven.'

'Thank goodness I'm close to retirement.'

'We should celebrate with a trip, don't you think?'

'Yes, but no cruises, because you get all the suitors.'

I improvise dinner for two. Tomorrow will be another day.

When I drive I listen to classical music. A listener calls in to say that his dog is a fan of Beethoven's *Pastoral*. The goldfinch of a follower of the program sings more joyfully while it listens to Boccherini's *Minuet*. Someone requests Nabucco's *Chorus of the Hebrew Slaves* for his recently deceased guinea pig.

The times I wanted to slap Colette! He erased a whole story I'd written once, when he walked all over my computer. Poor thing, he was bored with me. I still keep his collar and the sound box with the seagull squawks in a drawer. I listen to it from time to time.

I liked having a cat. He'd watch me from the top of the bookcase until he got fed up and jumped on top of the dictionary. I owned Ray Bradbury's quip: 'That's the great secret of creativity. You treat ideas like cats: you make them follow you.' Although it was the other way around, really.

I miss his welcoming purrs. When he was there it was like the light was always on at home. I'd scratch his chin seeking ideas and found questions: *Are you patient? Will you meet the challenge and adhere to the rules? What do you give priority to: truth, beauty, or goodness? Do you reflect on what you want to tell? Do you know that the search for the absolute – whatever that may be – is sometimes extinguished, dimmed down by its own obsession?'*

His photo on the desk has spurred me to continue. He kept me company while he lived, and with his death he announced that a time was coming to an end for me too, that it was time to open up to another, to an unavoidable phase of unknown destination.

The beautiful thing about life is how it forces us to move from the places where we are stuck.

It's black, the size of a peach. He scrunches his snout as if wanting to suckle. We almost stepped on it while crossing Abaroa Park. It was T. who noticed him.

'They've abandoned him.'

She sets him down on the grass, but he stubbornly slides onto the gravel. One time. And another. He reminds me of myself, refusing to crawl on soft ground, choosing hard ground.

'What do we do?'

It's not a question.

We remember an anecdote from childhood: childhood friends are a reservoir of memory.

We once found a litter of kittens in a stairwell. We each adopted one and put them inside our shoes, covering them with our handkerchiefs, as if they were little babies in cradles. *The blond one for me, the stripy one for you, who'll have the black one...* We petted them as much as we wanted. When we returned to the stairwell the following day with some treats for them, I stepped on something soft that burst like a ripe fig and left my white socks mottled with blood. The dim light of a bulb revealed the mother eating her last kitty.

'What do we do with this little one?' she insists. 'He could be Colette's replacement.'

No. The reverse of abandonment is constraints.

'There's nothing to do,' I reply. And we continue walking towards the lighthouse.

On the way back we walked into Miramar. Lemons and cala lilies. T. leaves; I don't: today is a good day for a bonfire.

I feel my elders in the trees, in the plant pots, in the tools. I imagine your conversations, dear voiceless bones.

This January afternoon is so bright that it hurts my eyes.

My operation is now behind me: a scaffold has been nailed into my eye socket, my eyelids have been trimmed and sewn up, and the worn silicone has been cauterised.

I wear a pirate patch until the stitches heal.

But enough of this business: I have already awarded literary attention to my lost eye in another book. I don't want to lend this particular event any extraordinary meaning.

Freedom can begin with a match.

I set fire to the stubble pile. This way of saying goodbye,

or it's over, or *the end*, doesn't make me feel like a goddess. I would like it to.

There is no lack of brambles, rubbish, stones and roots occupying a place that doesn't belong to them. Nothing will rise from the ashes, much less a phoenix. Never mind that, they'll do to fertilise the plot.

The other pyre – of debits and credits, of successes and mistakes, of legitimate and illegitimate steps – I have developed on paper, a combustion nourished by true life and feigned life.

Everything is process, everything is writing.

To finish this text off has supposed the culmination of an act of liberation from a sad and lethargic Ferris wheel.

My son shows up unexpectedly.

'Have you run your errands?'

'Yes, I'm here to help you.'

My son is unbelievable.

I feel my wrinkles, my capitulations, my enigmas, my fears, my secrets, my tears, my duels, my weaknesses, my faults, my mistakes.

'Are you crying?'

'No, it's because of the smoke.'

'Seriously, Ama, how are you?'

'Onward, always.'

Our motto.

'I'm in the trench with you. Not everyone does what you've done.'

'What have I done?'

'What animals do when they fall into a trap.'

I hug him.

Oh, you fool, I tell myself, sorrows don't last a hundred years. If you weren't who you are, yesterday's girl, today's woman, dancing to the sound of gut feelings... You bring your skin, your hands, your eyes, your bones onto the dance floor after making them wait their turn in your guest list.

Dusk settles.

The sunshine fills my hair and dreams hang in the air...

Someone's music is playing very loud in the building across.

It's a wonderful, wonderful life...

Listen, the last testament.

So I leave it here and now with this full stop and Colette under the fuchsias. In Miramar, on January 29, 2019.

PARTHIAN TRANSLATIONS

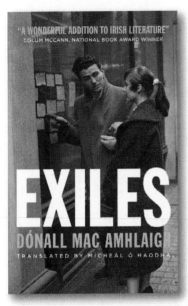

EXILES
Dónall Mac Amhlaigh

Translated from Irish
by Mícheál Ó hAodha

£12.00
978-1-912681-31-0

HANA
Alena Mornštajnová

Translated from Czech
by Julia and Peter Sherwood

£10.99
978-1-912681-50-1

Creative
Europe

LA BLANCHE

Maï-Do Hamisultane

Translated from French
by Suzy Ceulan Hughes

£8.99
978-1-912681-23-5

THE NIGHT CIRCUS
AND OTHER STORIES

Uršuľa Kovalyk

Translated from Slovak
by Julia and Peter Sherwood

£8.99
978-1-912681-04-4

A GLASS EYE

Miren Agur Meabe

Translated from Basque
by Amaia Gabantxo

£8.99
978-1-912109-54-8

Creative
Europe

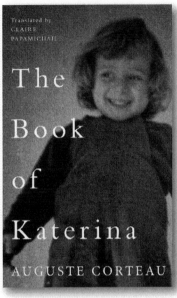

THE BOOK OF KATERINA

Auguste Corteau

Translated from Greek
by Claire Papamichail

£10.00
978-1-912681-26-6

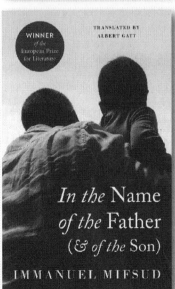

IN THE NAME OF THE FATHER (& OF THE SON)

Immanuel Mifsud

Translated from Maltese
by Albert Gatt

£6.99
978-1-912681-30-3

Creative
Europe

HER MOTHER'S HANDS

Karmele Jaio

Translated from Basque
by Kristin Addis

£8.99
978-1-912109-55-5

WOMEN WHO
BLOW ON KNOTS

Ece Temelkuran

Translated from Turkish
by Alexander Dawe

£9.99
978-1-910901-69-4

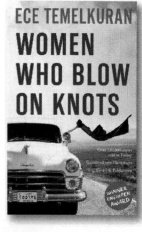

THE HOUSE OF
THE DEAF MAN

Peter Krištúfek

Translated from Slovak
by Julia and Peter Sherwood

£11.99
978-1-909844-27-8

Creative
Europe

PARTHIAN TRANSLATIONS

DEATH DRIVES AN AUDI

Kristian Bang Foss

Winner of the European Prize
for Literature

£10.00
978-1-912681-32-7

FEAR OF BARBARIANS

Petar Adonovski

Winner of the European Prize
for Literature

£9.00
978-1-913640-19-4

PARTHIAN TRANSLATIONS

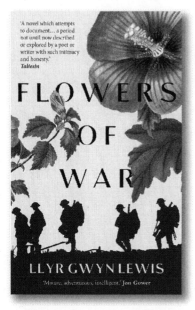

FLOWERS OF WAR

Llyr Gwyn Lewis

Short-Listed for Wales
Book of the Year

———

£9.00
978-1-912681-25-9

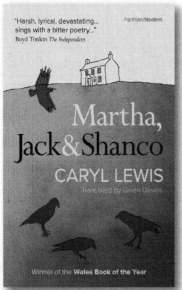

MARTHA, JACK AND SHANCO

Caryl Lewis

Winner of the Wales
Book of the Year

———

£9.99
978-1-912681-77-8